SCARED TO DEATH

The cemetery was filled with wispy mist, glowing with phosphorescent light as it twisted and curled into strange shapes. Standing in the middle, flailing and screaming in a frenzy, was Joe. As Frank watched, his brother sliced and smashed at the mist with a large shovel as though he were fighting demons. Joe's eyes were wild with panic.

"Joe!" Frank moved toward his brother. "Take it easy. Whatever they did to you, we can fix it," Frank said in a soothing voice.

"You, too?" Joe's voice was almost a whisper. "They got you, too?"

"Who?" Frank asked.

"Them!" Joe screamed, waving toward the enveloping mist around them. Then he rushed at Frank, his shovel held high. "They got you," Joe bellowed. "But you won't get me!"

He swung the shovel in a killing blow, aimed right at Frank's head.

Books in THE HARDY BOYS CASEFILES® Series

Available from ARCHWAY Paperbacks

THE HARDY BOYS CASEFILES NO. 80

DEAD OF NIGHT

FRANKLIN W. DIXON

AN ARCHWAY PAPERBACK
Published by POCKET BOOKS
New York London Toronto Sydney Tokyo Singapore

AN ARCHWAY PAPERBACK *Original*

An Archway Paperback published by
POCKET BOOKS, a division of Simon & Schuster Inc.
1230 Avenue of the Americas, New York, NY 10020

Copyright © 1993 by Simon & Schuster Inc.
Produced by Mega-Books of New York, Inc.

ISBN: 0-671-79464-7

First Archway Paperback printing October 1993

10 9 8 7 6 5 4 3 2 1

THE HARDY BOYS, AN ARCHWAY PAPERBACK
and colophon are registered trademarks of Simon & Schuster Inc.

THE HARDY BOYS CASEFILES is a trademark
of Simon & Schuster Inc.

Cover art by Brian Kotzky

Printed in the U.S.A.

IL 6+

Chapter

1

"HAPPY HALLOWEEN, HARDYS." The quiet voice came over the speakerphone. "I suppose you're wondering why I wanted to speak to you both at once. It's a treat, I promise, not a trick."

Frank Hardy ran a hand through his thick brown hair. "So this is why you dragged me away from breakfast and into the den," he said, glancing at his younger brother, Joe.

He recognized the voice on the phone, although its owner's real name was a mystery. The Hardys knew him as the Gray Man, an agent for a top-secret government intelligence force known as the Network. Mr. Gray, as he was sometimes known, looked like an insurance salesman while actually being an exceptional spy.

Frank and Joe had worked both with and against him, which was probably why the government man was promising no tricks.

"So what's the treat?" Frank asked suspiciously. He didn't altogether trust the man.

"You've just won an all-expenses-paid trip to Washington," the Gray Man said. "We're going to trial on the Ring of Evil case, and your testimony will be crucial."

Joe Hardy nodded. "So Boris's lawyers ran out of delaying tactics. Good. Maybe we can nail the slime."

"I'm glad you're so eager to take the stand," the Gray Man said. "We're depending on your testimony."

"I'm ready," Joe told him.

Frank gave his younger brother a sidelong glance. Joe might talk a good game, but to Frank he looked a little tired and sad.

The tired part Frank understood all too well. Instead of a vacation, the past summer had turned into a whirlwind of peril as the case they were following grew larger and more frightening.

At first it had seemed like a routine job, breaking up a small-time luggage theft operation at Atlanta, Georgia's Hartsfield Airport. But the Hardys had stumbled across a higher-stakes game involving the Network and the Assassins, a worldwide terrorist group.

Frank and Joe had tangled with the Assassins before. Even so, they were unprepared for the sheer horror of the plot they uncovered after a wild chase halfway around the world.

The Assassins had planned to detonate a hydrogen bomb inside an Indonesian volcano. The explosion would have triggered earthquakes and tidal waves, the terrorists knew, and literally would have changed the face of the world.

The Hardys had managed to defeat the Assassins, and help capture one of the terrorist survivors, a brutal thug code-named Boris. He'd been identified as an American named Thad Brubaker and now faced a variety of murder and conspiracy charges. Joe was assisting the prosecution with all his might. He had a personal reason. First, he had had the shock of discovering that a new friend, Gina Abend, was an Assassin. Then he had seen Boris kill her. Had he really gotten over it? Frank wondered.

"The trial is scheduled for next week, so clear your calendars," the Gray Man told them.

"So long as it's not tonight," Joe replied. "Frank and I have a date with two blonds and a boat."

"Have a good time," the government man said, chuckling. "And don't let the goblins get you."

"I'm *sooo* scared," Joe Hardy said to his brother as they hung up. "We'll be partying in a haunted house, and I'll just be a nervous wreck.''

"Yeah, me, too," Frank said, laughing at his brother's mocking tone. He looked at his watch. "Come on, if we're going to get scared out of our wits, we have to start getting ready.''

At three o'clock that afternoon, the Hardys were walking down Dock Street toward the Bayport boat basin with Callie Shaw, Frank's girlfriend. They had parked their van nearby. All three were carrying supermarket bags filled with potato chips, pretzels, dip, and other snacks for the party.

"I hope you've got a good ghost story or two ready," Callie told Joe.

"Oh, don't tell me we're going to do all that hokey stuff." The younger Hardy brother rolled his blue eyes. "Borrring," he drawled.

"It's traditional Halloween entertainment," Frank said, annoyed. The breeze off Barmet Bay ruffled Frank's dark hair, and he pushed it back with one hand.

"Look around you," Callie said. "Ghouls and ghosts are the way to go."

All the store windows around them were set with the usual symbols of Halloween: Indian corn and haystacks with goblins peeking from behind, Frankenstein monsters looming over several displays, vampires showing their fangs. Several stores were even decorated with spray-on cobwebs. And, of course, all the candy stores were doing a booming business in trick-or-treating supplies. Already children in colorful costumes were running up and down the streets, giggling and shrieking.

One little boy in a hooded costume came rushing up. Joe tried to dodge, only to have the trick-or-treater cannon into him.

"Watch where you're going, kid!" Joe said, laughing, as the costumed child rebounded into Frank's path, nearly tripping him.

Joe shrugged his broad shoulders. "Oh, boy, the wonders of Halloween. By the time that kid gets over his candy rush, they'll be redoing all the stores for Thanksgiving. Then, I suppose, you'll want me to walk around with a musket and a stupid Pilgrim's hat."

"Well, what's wrong with a Halloween haunted house party?" Frank wanted to know.

"It's just . . . old-fashioned," Joe finally said. "Ghost stories don't seem so impressive to kids who can go to the multiplex and see *Night of the Evil Blood Butcher, Part Six.*" He pointed to the downtown movie theater they were passing. On its marquee was an announcement for a Halloween Film Festival. The signs in the front display cases were all for horror films with high body counts.

"So you're saying that splatter films have spoiled Halloween?" Frank asked.

"Well, they make the old stories seem pretty tame in comparison," Joe said. "I mean, I am personally threatening to throw up if I hear that one about the maniac with the hook again."

"So you'd rather curl up with the VCR and slip in some creep show than go out to a Halloween party?" Callie laughed. "I would never have believed it. Joe Hardy turning into a couch potato!"

Frank was a little surprised, too. "I don't get it," he said. "You love action flicks, even though you've seen a lot more of the real thing than most people."

That was very true. Joe might be only seventeen and Frank a year older, but they'd investigated more mysteries, and gotten dumped into more foreign intrigues, than a lot of so-called professionals. Frank looked at Joe with concern. Maybe his younger brother was more tired than he had thought.

"There'll be fun enough," Frank said, trying to cheer his brother up. "We'll have a nice sail across the bay this afternoon, then the climb to the house on the cliff, and Frisbee and stuff until evening. And, of course, the cookout—"

"And finally, scary stories," Callie put in. "Think about it: the old dark house, a crackling fire, a cup of hot cider in your hand—"

"And your other arm around Vanessa Bender," Frank said, going for the clinching argument. "She's never seen that old mansion. And no matter how much you make fun of

6

ghost stories, they do make girls shiver and cuddle close."

Callie gave him a look. "Or so you hope."

Joe smiled. "Vanessa *hasn't* seen the old haunted house yet."

"You and Vanessa can explore it," Callie said to Joe. "I'll make sure Frank doesn't tag along as chaperon."

"It's a dangerous mission," Frank said, trying to look serious. "But if you choose to accept it . . ."

"I'll take some time alone with Vanessa," Joe said.

Frank was glad that Joe was now looking a little livelier. Usually, his blond-haired, good-looking brother was the party animal of the Hardy team.

Callie pulled Frank aside, pretending to show him a window display. "It seems like Joe really likes Vanessa," she whispered.

Vanessa Bender had enrolled at Bayport High only recently, but Frank had noticed Joe's interest in the pretty new student with the ash blond hair.

"Yes," Frank agreed, "and I think that might be good for him. He's been a little too wild and crazy since—" He paused for a second. "Since Iola."

Iola Morton had been Joe's serious girl-friend. But she'd been killed by a terrorist bomb.

"You're right," Callie agreed. "Vanessa

could be really good for him." She gave Frank a hug as they started to walk again. "I know we're *all* going to have a great time."

They caught up with Joe so all that he heard were the last words. "Yeah," he said. "We *will* have a great time. And I'm looking forward to seeing Vanessa."

Dock Street ended at the gates of the Bayport Marina, where several pleasure boats were being prepared for the Halloween party. Many of the Hardys' friends were on the piers. Off to one side, Tony Prito was loading his speedboat, the *Napoli*. Frank noticed Chet Morton carrying a big box of food aboard.

At least two other boats were being prepared, too. In the distance, at the last slip on the dock, was the good ship *Vanessa*. The Benders' cabin cruiser would be the biggest of the boats crossing the bay that afternoon. Mrs. Bender was an avid boater, as the Hardys had discovered. With the success of her animation studio, she'd splurged on a big boat.

Joe had been really impressed to learn that Vanessa had almost been brought up piloting craft in the waters around New York City.

"Hey, Joe," Frank said. "I think our captain is waving to you."

Sure enough, a blond-haired figure stood behind the windshield of the cabin cruiser's small bridge. Although the Hardys were still far away, Vanessa gave them an eager wave.

Then Vanessa brought her hand down to the control panel. A second later they heard the deep chug of the cabin cruiser's engine.

That throbbing note was suddenly drowned out by the roar of a horrifying explosion. Other vessels danced madly on a small, man-made tidal wave.

The *Vanessa*—and Vanessa Bender—vanished in a white-hot ball of flame.

Chapter
2

"No," Joe said at the first explosion. Then came a second blast, even stronger, nearly knocking them off their feet. A blazing fireball rose from the body of the burning vessel.

"Nooo!"

Joe dropped the bags he'd been carrying and raced down the long wooden pier.

He could hear Frank taking off after him. It would be like the time with the car bomb, Joe thought, when Frank hadn't let him get close enough to try to rescue Iola. Sure, the fireball might have killed him—probably would have, Joe had to admit. But didn't Frank understand he had to try?

Joe saw that the explosions had torn the *Vanessa* loose from its moorings. Frantic, he decided to make a running dive into the water, then swim to the burning hulk. Maybe there'd be a miracle. Maybe Vanessa would still be alive.

As he ran, Joe muttered, "Not again. Oh, please, not again."

Frank's slightly longer legs allowed him to catch up. He tried to grab Joe's arm, only to be angrily shaken off. "Don't try stopping me!" Joe yelled.

Frank knew he had to stop his brother before he plunged into the deadly flames. He went for a restraint hold, grabbing one of Joe's wrists and twisting it. Joe spun around, throwing a wild punch that grazed Frank's cheek. Joe tore loose and darted for the end of the pier.

"That does it!" Frank muttered. He hurtled into Joe with a flying tackle that brought them both down. A large splinter from the rough wooden boards tore at Joe's denim jacket as he tried to twist away.

Pieces of burning debris had fallen onto that section of the pier, and the fire was spreading. Joe could hear the crackle of flames nearby as he and Frank rolled back and forth, Joe struggling to get loose, Frank trying to hold him down.

Heat scorched Joe's back. Frank's hold slackened as he tried to avoid being pitched into the flames. Joe was free again!

But now other hands were grabbing him. Tony Prito, Chet Morton, Phil Cohen, and

Biff Hooper had joined Frank in holding Joe down. Thrashing, Joe almost wrenched himself free, but his friends restrained him, smothering his struggles. *"Nooo!"* His voice was more like a howl. "I've got to save her."

In the background he could hear people shouting and the approaching sirens of the harbor patrol.

"There's hardly anything left of the boat," Tony said, his voice gentle. "There's nothing—no one—to save."

The horror of going through this all again overwhelmed Joe.

It's a nightmare, he kept telling himself, his eyes clenched shut. I'm actually lying in bed having a bad dream. When I open my eyes, it will be morning, and everything will be all right.

But when he opened his eyes, he found himself still on the pier, encircled by his friends. At least they weren't holding him down anymore. Guess they think I won't do anything stupid, Joe thought.

Shakily he got to his feet. Three dock workers with extinguishers were putting out the fire on the pier. As for the *Vanessa,* the cabin cruiser had burnt down almost to the waterline. A fireboat was playing a stream of water over the smoldering hulk.

The sea breeze sent a cloud of acrid smoke their way, and Frank started choking and coughing.

Joe felt as though he were choking, too. But the stab of pain in his chest came from his heart, not his lungs. Vanessa had disappeared in a burst of flame and smoke. Just like Iola.

A husky, round-faced man in a blue uniform came up to the group. He looked vaguely familiar, Joe thought. Then he placed him. Inspector Herbert Fischer, the fire marshal for the harbor patrol. "I understand Miss Bender was aboard the vessel when it exploded. Was anyone else?"

Joe tried to speak, but he couldn't seem to get an answer out.

"I don't think so," Frank said. "We were the only ones who were supposed to be going with her."

"We'll inform the girl's parents," Fischer said.

"She only has—had—a mother," Joe managed to say. "She's away. Somewhere—somewhere in Europe on business."

The fire marshal sent a compassionate glance Joe's way. "We'll locate her, and we'll handle the official notification." The inspector turned to Frank. "Your brother doesn't look as if he's in very good shape. Take him home. I can interview you two tomorrow."

"Who did it?" Joe suddenly asked. "Who blew up the boat?"

"It could have been an accident," Fischer said. "We have no reason to suspect foul play, unless you can give us one."

13

"No," Joe said numbly. "No reason."

Joe insisted on staying and giving a statement to the harbor patrol. It was nearly an hour before Frank drove them all home. In the van Callie tried to console Joe, but she was in almost as bad shape as he was. Her eyes were blurry with tears, and her words of comfort came out in broken sentences.

"It's the shock," Joe found himself saying to her. "Just take it easy for a little while and you'll feel better."

"Exactly what I was going to say to you," Frank said, pulling the van up in front of the Shaws' house. He helped Callie out, then walked her to the door. She clung to him for a minute, then opened the door. Mrs. Shaw stood there, her face showing her shock as she heard the news. Joe could feel her glance as he sat alone in the passenger seat.

I got over Iola's death, Joe told himself, and I can get over Vanessa's. But his heart seemed to twist in his chest. He managed to rub the tears from his eyes with the back of his hand before Frank returned.

"Let's head for home," Frank said quietly.

The shadows were growing long when they reached the Hardy house on Elm Street.

"That's funny," Frank said. "The lights are on. They weren't when we left."

He opened the door, and a familiar voice called from the kitchen, "Oh, boys, I wondered where you were."

"Mom!" Joe said in surprise. "Why are you home? Why aren't you with Dad and Aunt Gertrude in New York?"

Mrs. Hardy put a hand to her stomach. "I've got some kind of virus. Your dad and aunt were having so much fun at that family get-together that I told them to stay and I'd come home early. I called to see if you boys were home. When I didn't get an answer, I took a taxi from the airport. I decided to leave the car in the car park for your dad and aunt."

"I'm sorry to hear you're sick," Frank said. "But I'm glad you're here. Something terrible has happened."

Mrs. Hardy's face showed her distress as Frank related what had happened down at the marina.

Joe just stood, rigid, as she gave him a gentle hug.

"Poor Vanessa!" his mother said. "And there's no chance that she—"

"None." Joe felt as though he had to force that one word through his throat.

"Oh, Joe, how awful for you." Even as his mother tried to comfort him, Joe noticed the worried looks passing between her and Frank.

What do they expect? Joe thought, a sudden surge of anger going through him. Do they think I'm going to go out and shoot myself? Okay, so I lost it a little on the pier. But that's over.

The anger passed, and now Joe only felt emptiness. It's *all* over now.

From the corner of his eye, Joe saw their mother gesture Frank away. Then she took Joe by the arm. "Why don't you come into the kitchen with me?" she asked gently.

Lined up on the kitchen counter were a number of round, pinkish orange clay jack-o'-lanterns, about six inches high. Each had a different face. Some looked scary, others were laughing. One pumpkin's lips were rounded in an O of surprise.

"I was puttering around when I got home, getting the jack-o'-lanterns all set up," Mrs. Hardy said, in an attempt to distract Joe. "I thought Frank would have had them out already. I remember how he fell in love with them the moment he saw them in the store. A little seven-year-old, pointing and begging that your father and I buy them."

Her smile grew a little sad. "You weren't with us that day. You were playing with a friend. We bought the jack-o'-lanterns and brought them home. You hated them! For years, whenever our backs were turned, you'd blow out the candles—"

"Mom," Joe broke in. "I know you're trying to help, but you don't have to worry about distracting me. I'm all right, really." He forced a smile as he looked at the pottery jack-o'-lanterns. "Although, to tell you the truth, I'm still not too wild about these dopey things."

"I'm sorry," Mrs. Hardy said. "I *was* trying to distract you." She hugged her son again. "But I want you to know that I'm here, if you need to talk."

"I know that already. Thanks, Mom."

Joe went back into the living room to find Frank looking out the front window into deepening darkness. "It's not even ten of five, and the sun's almost set." Frank glanced at his brother. "Some Halloween."

Joe's response was a brief nod. He couldn't get the vision of the explosion out of his mind.

Just then Mrs. Hardy called Frank into the kitchen for their annual ritual of lighting the candles and deciding which jack-o'-lantern went into which window.

Joe looked out the living room window at a group of children dressed in costumes. There were fewer hobos and princesses than he remembered from his own trick-or-treating days. A lot of the kids were dressed as slasher-movie monsters. He saw two Blood Butchers carrying shopping bags down the street.

Just then Mrs. Hardy walked into the living room, carrying a lit jack-o'-lantern. She looked out the window and saw the trick-or-treaters. "Oh, no," she said. "They'll be ringing the bell when they see the lanterns, and here we are without any treats! I can't put this in the window yet.'' She carried the lantern out of the room.

Of course, Joe thought. Frank and I weren't supposed to be here tonight. We were going to be across Barmet Bay with Vanessa.

His thoughts were cut off by the ringing of the phone. Joe picked up the receiver and said, "Hardy residence."

"You had someone new already, didn't you, Joe?" a girl's voice said. "You should have known it wouldn't last. Everything you touch dies, doesn't it? And more will die. Trust me on that, Joe. Tonight the dead will come for the living."

Joe stood frozen, the phone clutched to his ear. He knew the voice coming over the line. Once he'd eagerly waited to hear it on the phone.

But it was impossible that he was hearing this voice now. Totally impossible.

The voice was Iola Morton's—and she was dead.

Chapter

3

"WHO IS THIS? What do you want? Hello?"

Frank, walking into the living room, heard the wild note in Joe's voice. He saw his younger brother standing with the telephone clenched in his hand.

Joe seemed to be glaring into the receiver as if he could see the person on the other end. Every muscle in his face was pulled taut with strain.

"Iola—" The name came out almost as a cry of pain.

"You okay, Joe?" Frank asked. "You look as if you've just seen a ghost."

Joe turned, his face pale, his eyes staring. "I just heard one," he said in a hoarse voice. "That was Iola on the phone. She—she was mocking me about Vanessa's death."

"Joe—"

"She said, 'Tonight the dead will come for the living.' Then she hung up." He shuddered. "Frank, it was bizarre."

From the look on his brother's face, Frank thought a better word for it would be *chilling*. Joe was really spooked.

Frank shook his head. "It's a shame that people pull stuff like this for Halloween. They may think it's funny, but I think it's really sick."

At last Joe snapped out of his daze and slammed the phone down. "I wonder how funny they'd find my fists in their faces," he growled. Then he hesitated, glancing at the phone. "Weird, though. Whoever it was sounded just like Iola."

"I hate to say it, but you were well primed," Frank said. "If the caller sounded even halfway like Iola, that would have pushed your buttons."

"Iola or not, I don't like the way this girl said there would be more deaths." He repeated the rest of the girl's message.

Frank didn't like that, either. He remembered what had happened to Joe after Iola's murder—how he'd become quiet, grim, and scarily unpredictable. The best thing now, Frank decided, was to give Joe an outlet, a way to channel his grief.

The best distraction Frank could come up with was work. "Don't take it the wrong way when I say this, but maybe we should forget Iola and concentrate more on Vanessa.''

Joe looked at his brother. ''You're saying you don't think what happened on the boat was an accident?''

Frank shrugged. ''I'm saying I don't even know what happened on the boat. Maybe we should find out.''

''Treat it like a case, you mean. Yeah. Good idea.'' Joe frowned in thought. ''But who would try to kill Vanessa? She's pretty new in town. What enemies would a high school girl make? Who'd want to blow her up?''

Joe began pacing back and forth across the living room carpet. ''Now *we* were going to be on that boat,'' he went on, answering his own questions. ''What if someone set a bomb for us but it went off prematurely?''

Frank shook his head doubtfully. ''I don't know,'' he said. ''It's not like we've gotten any death threats.'' He paused for a moment, then added, ''It's a little early, but maybe we should call the cops and see if they've found anything yet at the blast scene.'' He grinned. ''And maybe you'd like to join me for a glass of milk and some cookies. I don't know about you, but I'm starved.''

Joe looked down at his body as if he were almost surprised to find it there. ''You know, I'm hungry, too.''

They went into the kitchen. "Where's Mom?" Joe asked.

Frank gave a half smile as he opened the refrigerator. "At the store. She came back into the kitchen all upset that we had nothing for the trick-or-treaters. I offered to drive her, but she said she wanted to walk."

"In that case, she lit the jack-o-lanterns too early," Joe said, pointing at the line of glowing faces. "I guess we'll wait to put these guys in the windows, since they're Mom's version of 'Come and get it!' for the neighborhood kids."

Frank set out milk and cookies for both of them, then said, "I think I'll call the police before I have my snack." He dialed the number of the Bayport police. "Frank Hardy for Con Riley, please," he said into the receiver.

Besides being an experienced cop, Officer Con Riley was the closest thing the Hardys had to a friend on the Bayport force. Frank hoped to get some information, right from the source.

The initial response wasn't encouraging. "Now, why was I expecting this little chat?" Con's deep voice came over the line. "Maybe the illustrious Hardy boys have a bit more to tell me than they gave Inspector Fischer? Perhaps about a case they've been working on? Chasing Patagonian tomb robbers or some such? A reason why someone would blow up a boat in our marina?"

Frank pounced. "So, there's evidence the boat was blown up?"

"There's not much evidence of anything," Officer Riley said, "because very little of the boat is left in one piece. Fischer is treating this as a suspicious occurrence, but he said it could be an accident. Maybe Vanessa Bender didn't air out the engine room—"

"And gasoline fumes accumulated in it and detonated when the engines started," Frank finished for him. "Dad had an insurance case like that once. As I remember, Dad also proved that someone could set that situation up. All it took was a warm engine and some spilled gasoline to vaporize into the air."

"You've got that right," Con said. "So, unless we find a piece of wreckage with the air vents closed, we aren't very likely to answer the *how* of what happened. That's why I'm asking you about the *why* of it."

"Let's not forget *when*, either," Frank said. "Joe and I were both about to get on that cabin cruiser."

"That's why I was hoping you could tell me something," Con Riley said.

"Con, there's nothing to tell," Frank assured the police officer. "We're not on any cases right now, and as far as I know, there are no loose ends from anything we *had* been investigating."

"Then it's an accident," Con said. "A tragedy. I hear that Joe had taken quite a liking to Ms. Bender. Just as he was very fond of Iola Morton. Is he getting along all right?''

Frank glanced over to where his brother sat at the kitchen table. Joe had his head cradled in his hands. He hadn't touched his glass of milk or plate of cookies.

"As well as can be expected," Frank said. "You might want to consider one other thing, Con. Vanessa had been boating for years. She was very well trained on boating safety. Does it seem likely she'd let herself get blown up that way?''

"Accidents happen," Con Riley said. "Otherwise, they wouldn't be called accidents. Right now we don't have any evidence to the contrary.''

Frank shook his head, feeling dizzy. Maybe it was all this roundabout discussion making his head spin. "Well, Joe and I are going to look into this," he finally said.

"Don't do it," Con Riley warned. Then he sighed. "I may as well not waste my breath with you two by talking about leaving police business to the police.''

"If we come across anything, we'll be sure to let you know," Frank promised.

"Well, isn't that public-spirited." Con's voice was full of sarcasm. "How nice of you to keep the proper authorities informed.''

Frank sighed. His head was beginning to throb. "Look. We *all* want to get to the bottom of this," he said.

On that, at least, Con Riley agreed. "Good luck, then," he said.

Frank thanked him, then hung up the phone. He ran a hand over his face as he sat down across from Joe at the kitchen table. "The police have nothing but a lot of questions," he said, relaying his conversation with Con.

Joe just sat where he was, nodding heavily. His snack still sat in front of him on the table, untouched.

"Lose your appetite?" Frank asked.

"Well, I don't see you digging in, either," Joe responded, pointing at Frank's glass and plate.

Before Frank could respond, Joe shook his head and said, "I don't know what it is, but all of a sudden I feel a little sick. Maybe I've got whatever Mom has. Or maybe . . ." He sighed. "Maybe it's just a reaction to what happened today."

Frank nodded in understanding. "To tell you the truth, I don't feel so hot myself. Kind of warm. And does the place seem stuffy to you?"

He went to rise from the kitchen chair, intending to open a window. Instead, he staggered and nearly fell. Grabbing hold of the table, he said, "Whoa! What—"

Joe leapt to help his brother and nearly collapsed on rubbery legs. "Something's wrong,"

25

he said in a hoarse voice. He was struggling to get his eyes to focus. *"Very* wrong."

"Got to get out of here," Frank said. The air in the room felt thick. It seemed to clog his throat, and he had to swallow several times to breathe.

Everything in the kitchen was wavering. It was as if the counters, furniture, and walls weren't real, but only reflections in a watery pond, a pond whose surface was being stirred by a strong wind.

Only the table under Frank's hands felt real, and even that was beginning to move. He shook his head, but the feeling only grew worse. They really had to get out of there.

"Back door!" Frank gasped. He wasn't even sure the words had made it out of his mouth. Joe's baffled-looking face seemed to loom very close, then suddenly slipped far away. "C'mon . . ."

Frank grabbed his brother's arm, and together they lurched from the table. Frank's legs didn't want to respond to the orders his brain was sending. They felt heavy, weighted down, and he couldn't seem to control them. He wanted to go to the kitchen door that led onto the porch. Instead, he and Joe staggered away from it, like a pair of drunken dancers.

Joe tottered as if he were walking on ice instead of kitchen tile. Then he was falling down, dragging Frank with him.

Maybe it was the fall or the cooler air down

by the floor, but Frank revived slightly. He shook Joe, who lay like a limp rag. "Som'-thin' bad hap'nin'," Frank said. "Gotta go."

He tried to push himself up, but the farther he got from the floor, the more giddy he became. Frank collapsed, unable to move.

"Help!" he tried to shout, but the word came out only as a thin croak.

Above him on the kitchen counter, the jack-o'-lanterns leered down at him. The dancing candle flames inside the pottery decorations flickered, making the faces seem to twist and mock him. Frank wished he had the strength to stand up and smash them.

Instead, everything went black.

Chapter

4

FRANK THOUGHT he heard bells—faint, distant bells—tinkling at him through a murky fog.

He wanted to follow them, but they kept drifting farther and farther away.

Some part of Frank screamed for him to move, to get up and run. But all he could do was drift into sleep and wonder why the thought of doing that terrified him.

Suddenly Frank was cold. The blackness around him seemed to sting like a thousand needles, as if he'd been dumped into a lake of ice.

But the cold also cleared his head and jarred him back to consciousness, up from the thick darkness that threatened to smother him.

Frank opened his eyes to find himself lying

in his backyard. He coughed and gagged. Just the effort of rolling onto his elbows sent a wave of nausea washing over him.

How did I get here? Frank wondered. The last thing he remembered was seeing the kitchen stretch and twist like a nightmare. He and Joe had fallen to the floor. Now he was outside and alone.

Frank blinked blurry eyes at the house looming in front of him. His vision cleared, and he could make out the two figures stumbling from the back door. He immediately recognized Callie Shaw's black jeans and leather jacket.

She wore a red and gold scarf across her face like a western bandit, and she was pulling Joe along.

"Joe!" Frank cried, his voice raspy.

Joe groaned in response but couldn't seem to focus on where Frank was. His body seemed clumsy, as if all it wanted to do was fall.

Got to get up and help, Frank thought. But his knees instantly folded beneath him, and he slammed into the cold, hard surface.

He lifted his head in time to see Callie and Joe drop down beside him.

Callie yanked the scarf from her face and gasped for air.

"Are you all right?" Frank asked as he was hit by another wave of dizziness.

"Sure." Callie coughed a bit, then gave him

29

a half smile. "Only next time you two have problems sleeping, try a glass of warm milk."

Joe tried to get up but quickly discovered moving was not a good idea.

"Lie still for a minute," Frank told him. "The dizziness will pass." Already he felt his own balance returning. He sat up and stared into the kitchen, through the open back door.

The jack-o'-lanterns sat on the countertop, leering back at him with a shimmering eeriness.

"What hit us?" Joe asked. "I feel like I've been swallowing cotton balls."

"Don't know," Frank said. He turned to Callie. "And what brings you here? Not that I mind."

"After what happened on the docks, I thought you guys shouldn't be alone tonight," Callie told him. "I figured I'd drop by to see if I could be of any help. You didn't answer the bell, but the front door was unlocked, so I came in."

"And found us sprawled out on the kitchen floor," Frank said.

Callie nodded. "Suddenly I started choking. I thought there was a gas leak. I slipped my scarf over my face, and, well, the rest you know."

"You saved our lives," Joe said as he sat up slowly.

"No kidding," Callie said.

Frank rose, reaching for Callie's bright red

and gold scarf. "May I borrow this?" he asked. "I've got a feeling it wasn't a gas leak that knocked us out. At least, not *natural* gas."

Joe tried to follow his brother, but he was still unsteady. He watched as Frank moved toward the house. "You've got a hunch?"

"I do," Frank replied from the porch. His gaze fell on the jack-o'-lanterns. "I sure do."

Once inside, Frank extinguished the candles. He quickly opened all the windows and doors, then went back out on the porch.

A few minutes later, the Hardys and Callie stood in the center of the kitchen.

"That was no gas leak," Frank said, pointing to the jack-o'-lanterns. "With the lit candles, we'd have had a gas explosion."

He picked up one of the pottery figures and looked at the candle inside. "Which means someone may have used these candles to try to kill us."

"I thought poisoned candles went out with old detective stories," Joe said. "Maybe we should get these over to the police lab and let them run a few tests. There could be side effects."

"What do you mean?" Callie asked.

"We've dealt with enough deadly gases to know that few things wash clean from your system," Joe explained. "There's always the chance of some kind of lingering effects. Sickness, hallucinations—stuff like that."

"Joe's right," said Frank. "But before we go, let's check out the house thoroughly. If there are any more traps, I want to find them instead of Mom finding them."

Joe's eyes widened. "That's right," he replied. "She was home before us, alone." He looked sick. "If she had lit those candles—"

He bit the words off. "What are we waiting for?" he demanded, hurrying to search the living room.

Callie looked worried. "Do you think he's going to be all right?"

"Joe can take care of himself," Frank told her, but he wasn't as sure as his words implied. "Maybe you'd better wait outside while we search." Callie shot Frank a "Get real" look. Frank smiled. "It was just a thought."

Frank and Callie went to search the den. Carefully they checked the light switches for possible booby traps. Frank was examining the heating vents when the phone rang.

He picked up the receiver on the second ring, but Joe was already on the living room extension. Frank heard his brother's greeting. Then he heard the other voice.

"It hurt, Joe," the voice was saying. "Did you know it hurts when you burn to death? When your flesh cooks—"

"Who is this?" Joe shouted into the phone. "Tell me who you really are so I can come over and show you how funny I think this is!"

"You know who I am, Joe. I loved you, and you let me die. Just like Vanessa."

In the living room, Joe's anger mounted. "You're not Iola! You're just some loony into sick jokes—"

"It's our night. The night of the spirits," the voice on the phone whispered. "There are so many of us here because of you, Joe. How many times have you cheated death? How many others have to die for you, Joe? Join us now, before we take another innocent."

"Like Vanessa?" Joe raged. "Like you took Vanessa this afternoon?"

The only answer Joe received was a soft click, then the steady drone of the dial tone.

In the den, Frank stared at the phone for a moment, then put down the receiver.

"What's wrong?" Callie asked, seeing the distressed look on Frank's face.

"Joe just got a crank call," Frank told her. "Go in there and calm him down. I'll be along in a minute."

As Callie hurried from the room, Frank's mind was racing. Had he really heard the voice of Iola Morton? Or was it just an excellent imitation?

Frank didn't believe in ghosts, but he did believe in evil doubles. He and Joe had encountered clones of themselves, impostors created by a perverted fusion of surgery and implanted computer memory.

Scientists at a place called the Lazarus

Clinic had perfected the technique of turning anyone, including foreign agents, into a nearly foolproof twin, with the looks, voice, even the memory of the original. To finance their own twisted agenda, they had hired out their services to the Assassins, fabricating a double of Iola.

That clone had nearly lured the Hardys to their deaths. But in the end, Frank and Joe helped the government smash the clone ring.

Or had they? Could the person tormenting Joe over the phone be someone repackaged as Iola Morton?

Frank picked up the phone and dialed the secret contact number for the Network. After giving the proper coded greeting, Frank was put through to the Gray Man.

"I thought you two had plans for the evening," came the voice of their Network contact.

"We did," Frank answered. "But someone has bigger ones." Frank quickly brought the Gray Man up to date. The government agent said little, but Frank could tell he was very interested, especially when Frank mentioned the Lazarus case.

"Their clinic in Maine has been shut down for some time now," the Gray Man told Frank. "It's dead up there."

"Then the dead must be walking," Frank replied grimly. "And it sounds like they're coming to Bayport. Can you guys check it out?"

"I can have people up there tomorrow," came the reply. "I'll even go up myself."

"Why not tonight? Joe and I could meet you in Maine."

"Tomorrow." It was an order, not a suggestion.

"Okay, then," Frank said evenly. "We'll see you tomorrow."

"Secure yourselves and stay put until then," said the Gray Man. Then he hung up.

Frank had no intention of waiting for the next day. Whatever was going on, Joe was the target, and there was no time to waste.

Joe was sitting on the couch with Callie as Frank entered the living room.

"Callie told me you heard the phone conversation," Joe said. "Now do you believe me?"

"I believe that call might tie into a case we had once—in Maine." Frank glanced at Callie. Even though he trusted her completely, he couldn't reveal their connection to the Network.

Joe caught on immediately. "You really think so? I thought the place was pretty much destroyed."

"Maybe not as much as we thought," Frank replied. "It's worth looking into."

"Are we going to get any help?" Joe asked.

"Not till tomorrow."

Callie raised an eyebrow. "All right, you

35

two. Quit beating around the bush. What's this all about?''

"There's this gang we smashed a while back.'' Frank quickly told Callie a bit about the case. He left out the Iola, Network, and Assassin connections.

"And you think they called you from Maine?'' she asked.

"I think Joe and I should check out their old hideout. It will be easier to catch them there than to wait for them to slip up here.''

"I agree,'' Joe said. "But what if you're wrong? What if this has nothing to do with them?''

"At least it gets you away from whoever is after you.''

"And it leaves Mom, and anybody else here, at their mercy. I couldn't handle another—'' Joe didn't finish the thought. "No. You go check it out. I'll stay here. That way I can have Con Riley test the candles, and I can keep an eye on Mom.''

Frank didn't want to leave his brother alone, but he had to agree that someone should watch over their mother.

"Okay,'' he said, grabbing the phone. "I'll charter a plane and see if I can get a car up in Maine. With luck, I can be up there and back by midnight. My old flight instructor, Rick Meyerhold, will rent me a plane.''

A minute later he was speaking into the phone. "Rick, it's Frank Hardy. I'm on a case and have to get somewhere fast. Can I charter your twin Cessna? Great! It's all gassed up? I'll see you in about half an hour.''

It took a couple of calls to arrange a rental car up in Maine, but Frank managed it. ''They'll have it waiting at the airport,'' he told Callie.

''Impressive,'' she said. ''I have only one change for your plans.''

Frank's brow creased. ''What's that?''

''You said you were going alone. But you'll have company. Me.''

Frank argued, but Callie would not give in. Finally she said, ''Look, we're wasting time with all this arguing. I'm going. That's it. End of discussion.''

Frank surrendered, and soon he and Callie were in her car, heading for the Bayport airfield.

''I hope Joe will be all right,'' he fretted as they pulled up in front of the airport terminal.

Callie turned to Frank. ''Funny,'' she said, and gently touched his cheek. ''I was thinking the same thing about you.''

He gave her a quick kiss, then said, ''Rick's operation is in hangar five.'' Frank pointed to a low one-story structure at the far end of the field.

Callie pulled up to the large hangar doorways and cut the engine. They both got out of the car. As they were about to enter the hangar, Frank caught her arm. ''Callie, I don't want you to go. I hate relying on instincts, but this whole thing feels dangerous, as if death will be all around us.''

''And I'll be safer here in Bayport.'' Callie sighed. ''I doubt it, but I give up.'' Impulsively she removed her scarf and offered it to Frank. ''Okay, Red Baron. At least take this with you.''

''Like the knights of old.'' Frank tucked the scarf into his jacket pocket, kissed her, then smiled. ''I'll give you a call when I get back tonight.'' He turned and walked into the hangar. She stood, watching him walk away.

The hangar was well lit by overhead lights, and Frank noticed that crates and boxes were stacked around the room.

A twin-engine Cessna was sitting in the center of the room. Its sleek, two-tone body was an impressive sight, and Frank couldn't wait to get behind the controls. But as he neared the plane, he suddenly felt uneasy. ''Hey, Rick?'' he called.

He glanced back toward Callie. She raised her hand to wave at him, then suddenly shouted, ''Look out!''

Frank whirled around in time to see a large fist coming straight for his head. He tried to twist out of the way, but he caught the blow on his shoulder.

The impact was painful. It sent Frank smashing up against the plane. Then he sprawled to the floor. Frank looked up. Towering over him was a huge man with deep-set eyes, very pale skin, and sharp, gaunt features. He was dressed entirely in black.

The man's powerful hands closed around Frank's throat in a viselike grip, as cold as ice, as cold as death itself.

Chapter

5

THE MAN'S FACE was expressionless as he increased the pressure on Frank's throat. Frank clawed futilely at his attacker's fingers. Tiny black spots began to float before his eyes, and he felt certain his life was over.

Suddenly he heard a loud crack. Startled awareness blazed in the man's eyes. For a second his grip loosened, and he swayed unsteadily.

Frank saw Callie Shaw standing behind his assailant, a broken board in her hand.

In that instant Frank lashed out. With steel-hard fingers, he jabbed at the man's windpipe. The attacker fell backward, and Frank quickly rolled away from him.

The man recovered just as quickly. He rose to his feet and started for Frank, who was still on his knees gasping for air.

Callie lunged at the man in black, trying to knock him off balance, but the man was too strong. He grabbed Callie and with the same cold expression flung her into a stack of boxes. Callie moaned and slumped to the floor.

Fury raged in Frank Hardy. He leapt to his feet and shot a high side kick to the attacker's jaw. The big man stumbled back but didn't fall. The blow seemed to have little effect. His face didn't even change expression.

The man in black advanced again. Frank fired off several rapid punches to the man's ribs, but again there was little reaction, as if his attacker had no feelings.

This is like fighting a zombie, Frank thought.

The silent assailant suddenly backhanded Frank, knocking him to the ground. Frank knew he couldn't take another blow like that. His jaw ached and his head reeled.

The man reached for Frank, who rolled out of his grip and sprang to his feet. Without a moment's hesitation, Frank ran straight for his attacker, landing both feet on the man's chest.

The impact sent the man staggering back into a large stack of crates. The heavy boxes collapsed, burying him under their weight.

Frank staggered over to Callie's side. "Sit still. I'll send for a doctor," he told her.

"Don't bother," Callie told him. "He just knocked the wind out of me." Callie looked up at Frank. "So, I'll be safe in Bayport, huh?"

Frank started to apologize, but Callie placed her finger on his lips. "Don't, Frank. It comes with the territory if you date a Hardy."

Frank smiled as he helped Callie to her feet. "Where's tall, pale, and gruesome?" she asked.

"Over there." Frank pointed to the pile of boxes. "I'd better make sure he's out cold before we get the cops, though. Maybe now we'll get some answers to this mystery."

But the search through the crates produced more questions than answers. The big man was gone. But they did find a dazed Rick Meyerhold.

"I was checking out the plane when this big ox comes up and decks me without a word," the pilot said.

"I guess he stashed you behind these boxes," Callie said. "But where'd he go?" She glanced at Frank.

Frank stared down at the pile of crates. "I don't know."

"So, what do we tell the police?"

"I'll let Rick decide that." Frank took Callie by the hand and started toward the hangar doors. "You go home—"

"No way!" Callie pulled away from Frank to stand with her hands on her hips. "I go along."

"I can handle this alone."

Callie pointed to the splintered board she'd used on their attacker. "Sometimes we all can use a little help. Even the famous Frank Hardy."

Frank had to admit that Callie had come through tonight, as she had in the past. And maybe leaving her alone wasn't such a good idea. If their attackers had killed Vanessa, would Callie really be safer in Bayport?

"Okay," Frank said finally. "But we play this my way. Right?"

"Don't I always?" Callie teased. "Let's go."

With Rick's help, Frank quickly checked over the plane. Moments later he and Callie were soaring into the skies, heading northeast.

"It's about five hundred miles to Allagash—a two-hour flight in this baby," Frank said. "That will get us there about nine o'clock. The old clinic is less than a half hour away. We can check it out and still be home not much after midnight, with luck."

With luck, Frank repeated to himself. But then, luck had not favored them so far—certainly not his brother, Joe.

The streetlights were glowing and the old clock tower was ringing out seven-fifteen as Joe Hardy pulled his van up in front of police headquarters. Merchants were trying to close up their shops, interrupted by swarms of trick-or-treaters.

Candy vampires, Joe thought with a wan smile as a group of kids burst out of a store, loudly comparing their take of goodies.

He remembered his own trick-or-treating days—the jokes, the spooky stories, stuffing his face with candy until he felt sick.

But on this Halloween, as he carried the jack-o'-lantern candles into the police station, Joe felt true evil in the air. And it was definitely looking for him.

"Joe!" a voice called. It was his friend Phil Cohen. Carrying a bulky package, he dodged a group of kids heading toward the stores for their last treats.

"I'm glad to see you're okay," Phil said a little hesitantly.

Joe realized that Phil had been going along with them to the haunted house party that afternoon. He was also among those who had held him down after the explosion.

Trying to lighten things up, Joe asked, "So, what's this? Additional supplies for hungry little goblins?"

"It's a piece of lab equipment I ordered. Since all our plans got, uh, changed, I figured I'd pick it up."

Yeah, Joe thought sadly, a lot of plans got changed when Vanessa was murdered. On impulse, Joe handed Phil one of the candles. "You've got quite a chemistry setup, don't you? Maybe you can take a look at this. But don't light it! There could be dangerous effects.''

After hearing a quick description of what the smoke had done, Phil said, "I'll be glad to check it out." He put the candle in his jacket pocket.

"Great. I'm giving the rest to the cops." Joe nodded toward the station entrance.

"Well, you take it easy," Phil said, heading for his car.

"Right."

At least he didn't wish me a happy Halloween, Joe thought as he mounted the stairs of the police station and entered.

"What can I do for you?" Con Riley asked from behind the front desk. "Everything all right?"

Joe found himself resenting the sympathetic tone. First Phil, now Con, he thought. I wish people would stop treating me as if I'm about to go off the deep end.

He held out the candles. "Could your lab check these out?' he asked gruffly.

Con scratched his head. "Any particular reason?"

"They might be laced with something," Joe replied. "Some kind of sleeping drug or maybe something more lethal. Frank and I nearly passed out from the fumes these things gave off."

"You two working on something the police should know about?"

45

"The only thing we're working on is why Vanessa Bender died." Joe winced as the image of the explosion suddenly flashed before his eyes.

Con leaned forward over the desk, his voice almost gentle. "The fire marshal hasn't ruled out an accident as the cause of the explosion. What makes you think these candles are tied in?"

Joe slammed a hand on the desk. "I don't *know* if they tie in. All I know is what happened to Frank and me when the candles were lit."

"Our lab people have a full schedule," Con said.

"So, when do you think they'll get to it?" Joe demanded.

"As soon as they can." Con's eyes locked with Joe's. "Look, I know you want answers, the sooner the better. You want someone to blame. Just don't let what happened today"— Con searched for the right words—"get to you. I mean, don't blame yourself."

"Sorry I can't stick around for the sermon, Con, but I have to get back home," Joe said angrily. "My mother went out to the store, and I expected her back a while ago."

Joe stormed away from the desk and out the front doors only to stop at the top of the steps and shake his head. "Why was I so rude to Con?" he said softly. "He's always been fair with Frank and me. Better get my act together.''

He walked down the steps toward his van, thinking about what the police officer had said.

Am I looking for someone to blame? he wondered. What difference does it make if Vanessa was killed by someone trying to get to me?

Joe slammed his fist into the side of the van. She'll still be dead. Just like Iola.

Slowly Joe walked around the van to the driver's side. He glanced across the street—and froze. There, standing in an alley and staring at him, was a slender, pixie-faced young woman wearing tight jeans, a turtleneck sweater, and a leather jacket. Her dark hair blew wild in the autumn wind.

Joe couldn't believe it. The girl was Iola. Or was she? She looked like Iola, but even from across the street Joe could see that her skin was almost white. She looked like a marble statue—or a ghost.

Iola Morton beckoned to him. Then she faded away into the darkness behind her.

Joe's legs didn't seem to belong to him as he sprinted across the street and entered the alley.

The moon had drifted behind some clouds, and the position of the buildings created a deep, narrow, shadowy pit. Joe couldn't see a thing as he blundered forward.

He'd taken only a couple of steps when an ethereal voice called to him. "I warned you, Joe, but you wouldn't listen. Now we'll have to take someone else."

"Wait a minute!" Joe shouted. His voice echoed down the alleyway. "What do you want? If you're really Iola, then you know how I felt about you! You know!"

No answer.

He walked a few steps farther into the alley, but no one was there. Feeling a bit dumb, Joe headed back toward the alley entrance. Someone else, he thought, puzzled. Did they mean Frank or—

The answer hit Joe like a blinding white light. He ran back to the van as fast as he could, jumped in, and put the key in the ignition.

Joe drove the van through the streets of Bayport at top speed. Still, that wasn't fast enough for him. Everything—the van, the traffic lights, even his own reactions—seemed to move in slow motion.

Despite the cool temperature, Joe felt beads of sweat breaking out on his face. He accelerated. "Home," he said through gritted teeth. "Please let me get there in time!"

The van screeched to a halt in front of the Hardy house, and Joe was out the door and up the driveway.

He burst through the front door and hit the wall switch. Nothing.

Joe flicked the switch on and off several times, but the lights didn't come on.

"Mom!" he called out.

Only silence greeted him.

She could have been back from the store a long time ago, Joe told himself.

He reached to turn on a table lamp in the living room. Nothing. He tried another light, then blundered on into the den, knocking over a floor lamp there. He didn't bother to try that one. He went, instead, to the desk lamp. Again nothing.

Frantic, Joe moved from room to room downstairs, then upstairs, flicking switches, calling out. Everywhere he found only darkness and silence.

"Power must be out," Joe muttered, standing in his room. "I should check the fuse box." But where was his mother?

Joe drew a long, shuddering breath. The silence was starting to get to him. Then he heard music, a soft, tinkling sound.

"A music box," Joe whispered.

The melody was familiar, although he couldn't place it at first. It was from *Peter and the Wolf*. Then he remembered.

His grandmother's music box. Joe hadn't heard it in years. Not since his mother had put it in the attic.

Feeling his way in the darkness, Joe climbed the narrow stairs to the top floor. The attic door was locked.

That's strange, Joe thought. Mom and Dad usually leave the key in the lock.

Joe pulled out his pocketknife and unfolded the thinnest blade. The lock was an old-fashioned one—not that tough to pick.

His hands trembled as he worked the metal blade back and forth. The locked clicked, and he slowly pushed the door open.

Stepping inside, Joe scanned the cluttered, musty room.

The ceiling slanted down to two small locked windows, one at either end of the attic. Pale blue moonlight dimly illuminated stacks of books, old clothes, boxes, trunks, and retired toys.

In the center of the room was a rocking chair, its back to the doorway. On the floor beside it was the music box. The lid, covered in tapestry cloth, was open, and the melody filtered through the room.

Joe moved forward slowly until he reached the chair.

In the semidarkness, Joe saw his mother sitting there. "Mom," he said almost timidly. "What are you doing up here?"

Mrs. Hardy sat still and quiet.

Her hands lay unmoving in her lap, and her head hung low, just above her gold brooch. Then Joe realized the shiny ornate object was no piece of jewelry.

It was the hilt of a dagger buried deep in his mother's chest.

Chapter

6

JOE STUMBLED AWAY from the grisly scene in shock and horror, knocking over several boxes. Then he slumped to his knees, covering his eyes with both hands.

"Not Mom," he sobbed. "What did she do that you had to take her?"

"Everything you touch dies." The words he'd heard over the phone echoed in his mind. "Join us now . . . before we take another innocent."

Joe took several deep breaths, trying to steady himself. You have to be reasonable, he told himself. You can't afford to freak out now. You have to get through this. You have to.

But could he? Joe thought he might be losing his mind. Vanessa's boat had blown up.

The impossible phone calls. The candles. The ghost in the alley. Now someone had murdered his mother in the attic of his own house.

Joe could hardly breathe. It was as if the walls were closing in on him.

Gasping for breath, Joe raced from the room and slammed the door. He nearly tumbled down the stairs as he hurried to the living room. Lurching through the dark, he found the phone and started dialing 911. Then he realized that there was no dial tone.

All Joe could think of was that he had to get to the police. His head pounded as he stumbled out the front door of the darkened house.

Squeals of high-pitched laughter echoed on the street. To Joe the giggles had a gloating, mocking note.

"Shut up!" he yelled.

But there were no trick-or-treaters in sight. He could hear the rustle of windblown leaves in the sudden silence. And down at the corner, a single, small, hooded figure stared at him for a moment before disappearing behind a hedge.

So much for pulling myself together, Joe told himself. Got to get out of here. Bring the police. He jumped into the van and tore off.

But as Joe screeched through the intersection at Elm and headed for the center of town, he wondered if the police could do him any good anymore.

It was shortly after nine o'clock when Frank Hardy set down at the airfield in northern Maine. He radioed in his touchdown time to the control tower, then turned to smile at Callie.

"Right on schedule," he said. The night flight had been smooth and swift. He'd been pleased that he was able to keep the plane at its top speed of more than 260 miles an hour.

Callie opened the door and turned up the collar of her leather jacket to protect her neck and face against the wind.

"I can't believe how cold it is up here," she said, shivering as they walked across the field.

Frank snapped his denim jacket closed, then slipped an arm around Callie. "Hey, I don't mind a good excuse to get close."

"No complaints here," Callie replied.

At the terminal Frank made the arrangements to have the plane refueled, while Callie went off to find some food. Neither of them had eaten in hours.

The rental car waiting for them had been new when Frank was about two years old, but it started without a problem. "Good thing I remembered the storekeeper up here hired out cars," he said. "Joe and I used him the last time we were up here. He even remembered us and promised me the best in his fleet.''

"Right,'' Callie said, getting in the passenger side. "He probably remembered you as the guys who were such big spenders,'' she said, laughing as she closed her door. "That's why he gave you the best car.''

"Well, at least it's clean,'' Frank said, "and the heater works.''

A delicious smell filled the air from the paper bag Callie was holding. "What's that?'' Frank asked.

"Special of the day—sandwiches and hot chocolate,'' Callie told him.

"Eat first, drive later,'' Frank said, and reached into the bag for a sandwich.

During the ride to the Lazarus site, Frank and Callie tried to keep things light, but they hadn't forgotten the events that happened earlier. Frank was particularly worried about Joe. He'd called home from the airport, but no one answered.

Still, he managed a few jokes as they turned off the highway, leaving farms behind and taking a narrow road into rougher, forested land.

Pine trees loomed over the road, their needle-covered boughs creating a rampart of darkness. Branches of the taller trees almost met overhead, turning the road into a tunnel. Now and then moonbeams filtered through the branches in fragmented pools of light.

Finally, Frank steered the car onto a graveled road that led into a large circular clearing.

There sat the massive form of the Lazarus Clinic, a rambling stone mansion surrounded by a cyclone fence topped with barbed wire. The outside of the three-story building was badly charred, and many of the windows were boarded up.

Frank drove up to the gate. It was wide open, dangling precariously from bent and rusted hinges.

"I don't believe this place!" Callie exclaimed. "It's like something out of a horror film." She shifted closer to Frank. "You said some kind of crime ring used this place. What were they stealing, cadavers?"

"You could say that," Frank replied, trying not to sound too evasive as he parked. He was surprised that the structure was still standing. He and Joe had narrowly escaped with their lives during an explosion there.

Frank and Callie left the car and cautiously made their way through the gates and up to the massive iron-barred wooden door. The heavy door was also badly charred.

"It doesn't look like anyone has been here in a long time," Callie said. She glanced at the overgrown lawn and the boarded-up windows.

"At least not since Joe and I were here." Frank tried the ornate doorknob. The door creaked open. "The place was built by a nutty millionaire about ninety years ago, then it got turned into an asylum," he said as he led the way inside.

Callie stared at Frank. "Oh, that makes me feel *much* better."

Frank pulled a flashlight from his jacket and swept the room with the narrow beam.

They were standing in a reception area with a high ceiling and cathedral windows. The carved stone walls were covered with thick black soot, a result, Frank knew, of the explosion.

Several long corridors led to different wings of the building. The broad staircase leading to the upper floors was strewn with rubble.

"Maybe this will turn out to be a wild-goose chase," Frank whispered as they moved past a badly burned semicircular reception desk.

"Well, there sure isn't a welcome wagon. Which way?" Callie asked. None of the passageways looked inviting to her.

"There isn't much point in going upstairs," Frank said. "From the looks of that staircase, I doubt that anyone could make it up there." He pointed to a corridor on their left. "When Joe and I were last here, there were a number of laboratories down that corridor. Let's try that one first."

Frank and Callie cautiously moved down the hallway. It didn't take them long to realize they had entered a maze. Hallway after hallway met in a confusing series of twists and turns.

Frank's penlight threw a narrow beam that barely penetrated the gloom. Now and then moonlight filtered in through narrow, barred windows. Frank noted that this part of the Lazarus place had been undamaged in the fire.

They listened at each door they came to, then tried the knob. Some were locked. Others opened easily, but the rooms were empty. Except for the skittering along the wallboards and an occasional flapping of wings overhead, the Lazarus Clinic was still and quiet. There wasn't a sign of activity anywhere.

After a while Frank was almost ready to admit his theory was wrong.

"The place really does look abandoned," Callie said nervously.

Frank ran the light along the floor in front of them. Nothing. No tracks.

"Maybe so," he replied. "But—" Just then they heard a strange sound from somewhere up ahead, a grinding noise like the sound of a hundred bones cracking.

Callie shivered. "We're going to check that out, right?" she asked hesitantly.

"*I* am," Frank said firmly. "Whatever it is, it's around that corner up ahead. I'll take a look. You stay here."

Frank felt sure Callie would be safer staying behind and waiting. The last turnoff they'd passed was fifteen feet behind them. Only two doors were close by, both locked.

If something was waiting beyond the corner, Frank could hold it off while Callie ran.

"I don't like this." Callie squeezed Frank's arm.

"Neither do I."

Frank turned off his flashlight. It would give him away as he advanced, maybe even be—he shuddered—a dead giveaway.

He moved cautiously along the hallway until he reached the corner. The sound was louder. He took a deep breath and suddenly whipped around the bend.

The sound stopped.

Ahead of him, the hallway went on for a hundred feet. In the moonlight from a window at the far end, Frank could see the area was empty. He strained to hear. The grinding sound had stopped, but he heard other, very faint sounds: scratches, clicks, creaks, whispers, a stifled scream.

The scream hadn't come from in front of him. It came from the corridor where he'd left Callie, alone.

Frank switched on his flashlight and ran back the way he'd come. Callie was gone.

"Callie!" he shouted. No answer.

Frank froze, listening. There wasn't a sound, not in any direction. No scuffling or cries.

They couldn't have disappeared down the hallway that fast, Frank told himself.

He eyed the two locked doors. The only

way was through one of them, he thought. But which one? Frank leapt to the first door and tried the knob. It was still locked.

He ran his flashlight along the doorjamb. Nothing. No marks of any kind.

He darted across the hall to the other door. "Give me a sign," he muttered desperately. "Something to show which one." Frank didn't want to waste time picking the wrong lock.

His flashlight beam traced along the doorjamb. He saw a scuff mark on the floor.

"That wasn't there before," Frank said softly, pulling out his lock pick.

Quickly he set to work. The lock was a standard security type, guaranteed to keep out the average thief or intruder. Frank was neither.

In seconds he was on the other side of the door, staring down a flight of rubber-tiled stone stairs. The basement, Frank thought. He moved quickly down the staircase, desperately hoping to catch up with Callie.

At the bottom he put away his flashlight and proceeded in the darkness down a narrow stone hallway to a single door at the far end.

Perfect setup for a trap, Frank thought. Suppose the door was electrified? With no shelter on either side of the hallway and the staircase twenty feet behind him, Frank also knew he was an easy target.

Frank shrugged off the thought and grabbed for the handle. He had to find Callie.

Frank whipped open the door and leapt inside.

For a moment he was still in darkness. Then a brilliant glare flooded the room from a set of overhead spotlights.

Halfblinded, Frank struggled to take in the scene. The chamber was large and bare, with dirty gray walls. In its center was a thick wooden table like a medieval torture rack. It was the focus of the blazing lights. It looked like the set from a show—a horror show.

Callie Shaw was strapped to the table by thick leather belts. Her gold and red scarf was tied around her mouth as a gag.

Above her, suspended from a rope and pulley somewhere in the ceiling, a huge blade swung back and forth, cleaving the air just inches above Callie. With every swing, it dropped a little closer, threatening to slice her in two, from head to toe.

Frank lunged forward into the blinding light, determined to cover the short distance and free her before it was too late.

As suddenly as the lights had gone on, they went off again. Frank stumbled against an obstruction at ankle level. A trip wire! he realized just a split second too late.

The wire snapped, and a net suddenly closed in around him, whisking him up off the floor.

As he was yanked into the air, the lights blazed on again and Frank heard a loud click.

He got a quick glimpse of the blade dropping. It took only a second for the blade to cut through its soft target and imbed itself into the table.

For Frank it seemed to take forever.

But Callie didn't even have a chance to scream.

Chapter

7

"THIS CAN'T be happening!" Frank Hardy yelled as he threw himself at the netting that entangled him. Just then the room plunged into darkness again.

Frank's brain shied away from the dreadful scene he'd just witnessed, the blood, the still form. He had failed Callie, and now she was dead. He was responsible. If he had insisted that she stay in Bayport . . .

Suddenly he was overwhelmed by anger. He had to find the people responsible for killing Callie. He would make them pay for what they had done. But first he had to escape. Using the largest blade of his pocketknife, he attacked the rubbery, sticky strands of the net that entrapped him. The strands resisted cutting. His blade sank halfway through, then

62

three-quarters of the way, and at long last a strand finally snapped.

Now on to strand number two.

The process seemed to go on forever. Each second was an eternity to Frank.

Eventually he severed enough of the cords to make an opening large enough to wriggle through. He tore his way out of the net, then paused in the darkness, halfway between the door to the chamber and the gruesome torture rack in the middle of the room.

One part of him wanted to rush over to Callie, to try something—anything—to save her. But a cold voice in his brain told Frank there was no help he could bring Callie. The blow of that monstrous blade had killed her instantly.

Still, I should go to her, Frank thought. Then his hands began to shake. Do I really want to see her this way? Do I even know it's safe to go over there? Maybe whoever created this little horror show is depending on that. Maybe another, more sinister booby trap is waiting to be sprung in the darkness over there.

Frank made up his mind and headed for the door. When he returned to this room, he'd bring help—official help—to nail the twisted sadists responsible for all this.

And when I get them, Frank vowed, they'll wish they'd never started to play this game. They'll wish they'd never been born.

Frank found the door and stumbled down

the stone hallway in near pitch-darkness, feeling his way. He was afraid to use his flashlight. He didn't want to make a target of himself.

As he forged his way down the narrow black corridor, Frank did his best to concentrate on escape. There were so many ways he could trigger another trap—pressure plates, trip wires, even undetectable electronic eyes.

He had no choice but to go on. Carefully, slowly, he crept up the steps to the main corridors. Once on the first floor, he kept his right hand on the moldy stone wall and moved ahead, retracing the twists and turns he'd taken.

At last he reached the outer reception chamber, lit by gleaming moonlight streaming in through the barred windows.

Heart pounding, Frank ran for the massive, iron-banded wooden door, which still stood ajar. He dashed across the overgrown lawn to the gravel road. His rental car was still there.

A thought flitted across Frank's mind. Should he check under the hood for any unexpected extras? What if whoever had killed Callie had planted a bomb?

Frank lifted the hood and quickly scanned the engine—nothing. Then he slammed the hood shut. Now was not the time to hang around.

Right, a little voice mocked him from a corner of his mind. Run away from it all.

I'm not running *from,* Frank thought. I'm running *to.* To get help. The only problem was, help was so far away.

Frank threw the car door open, got behind the wheel, and started the engine. The old car roared to life. Frank took it through a wild turn, skidding on fallen leaves and gravel as he pulled away. Through the rearview mirror he could see the ruins of the old madhouse eerily lit by the beams of a huge, orange, looming moon. Frank didn't even need the headlights until he reached the line of trees.

A ground mist was rising from among the trees, creating ghostly forms that swept across the narrow roadway. To Frank's imagination, they looked like Callie. There was Callie giving him a mischievous grin. He took a turn, and there was Callie again, her eyes wide with excitement.

Another turn, and he almost swerved into a tree. There was Callie, dead and butchered.

Frank floored the gas pedal, fleeing even faster through the haunted woods.

Joe always told me there was no way I could really understand how he felt after Iola died. Frank's lips were tight. His eyes burned with unshed tears. Now I see he was right.

Oh, Callie, he thought, I never should have listened to you. I should have never let you convince me. I should never have brought you here.

* * *

In Bayport Joe Hardy's thoughts were on his mother as he drove to the police station. Mom tried to comfort me when Vanessa died, and I pushed her away. She went off to the store, and I never had a chance to talk to her again.

He clenched his teeth together tightly, struggling to keep from crying as he drove. The residential section was still full of life. He braked to a screeching stop as a pack of older trick-or-treaters skittered across in front of him, looking like a collection of brightly colored leaves in his headlights.

It was almost nine o'clock, past bedtime for the really little ones. But the older kids were out in full force, up for any kind of prank. As he drove on, an egg whizzed across the street just in front of his windshield. At another corner two boys were squirting shaving cream on each other.

The closer he got to the downtown district, the less activity there was. At least they're not stupid enough to try any nonsense in front of police headquarters, he thought, pulling the van up in front of the building.

Joe took a deep breath, trying to calm himself. It wouldn't help to go in there raving like a maniac, he told himself. We'll just waste time while I convince them I'm telling the truth.

Con Riley was sitting behind the front desk. He had the phone to his ear and a harassed expression on his face. "You say they're T.P.-ing the house next door? We'll send a car around."

He rubbed a large hand over his square jaw, then got on the intercom. "More toilet-paper terrorists," he said, giving an address.

Then Con looked up and saw Joe. "Besides this juvenile crime wave, I've gotten three reports of Frankenstein roaming the streets and a lot of giggling telephone pranks. One of these days, we'll have automatic tracing on this line, and a lot of snotty little kids will live to regret it."

Then Con remembered what had happened to Joe. "I'm sorry," the policeman said. "The lab boys still haven't had a chance to get to those candles—" Con's expression changed as he looked more closely at Joe.

"Is there something more, Joe?" Con asked. "What's the matter?"

"Murder." Joe got the word out. "My mother—I found her in the attic."

"What?" The officer's face registered his surprise. "Isn't your mother supposed to be in New York? That's where your dad said they'd be when I bumped into him the other day."

"She came home this afternoon," Joe said. "Some kind of bug." The story poured out of him.

Con got on the intercom and made some arrangements. "If you don't mind, I'll be going on this call personally. I'd like Horvath to go along with me."

Joe followed the police car back to Elm Street. The closer they came to the Hardy house, however, the harder Joe found it to breathe.

The squad car pulled into the driveway, and Joe parked the van on the street. Con and the young police officer, Andy Horvath, waited as Joe came up to join them.

All the lights were still out. Officer Riley tested the doorknob. "Locked."

"I did that on the way out," Joe said. "So no one would disturb the evidence."

He slipped his key in, and the door swung open. Con's partner reached in, sweeping his hand over the light switch. Immediately the light clicked on.

"I thought you said the lights weren't working," the young officer said.

"They weren't," Joe said. "None of them went on."

They went slowly from room to room, checking the lamps. All of them lit.

"The crime scene is upstairs, correct?" Joe caught an odd tone in Con's voice as he said that.

"Yes, in the attic. I heard an old music box of my grandmother's and followed the sound up."

Silently Con led the way upstairs. They

paused at the attic door. Con turned the knob with care, then stepped inside.

Joe couldn't bring himself to confront that scene again. He stood at the bottom of the attic stairs, unable to go up and look inside.

A moment later Officer Horvath emerged, followed by Con Riley. Horvath's voice was serious as he said, "You ought to know that on Halloween there's always a tremendous drain on the department because of pranks."

What were they going to tell him? Joe wondered. That he'd have hours to wait before the crime scene crew would arrive? How could he stand to stay under this roof, knowing what was up there?

The young officer's features darkened as he walked down the attic stairs. "But to call us out on a phony-baloney murder case!" He broke off. "Pal, you've got a lot of nerve. And I'm going to make sure you explain that to a judge."

At that moment Con Riley grabbed the other policeman by the arm and whispered something in his ear.

For a second Officer Horvath looked as if he wanted to give Con Riley an argument. Then he shrugged.

"Joe," Con said quietly, "I know what happened this afternoon must have been a shock for you. And I really wish that your older brother hadn't been called away on business."

The officer kept his voice low and soothing. "Maybe you should try to get some rest."

"Rest?" Joe said, his voice rising a little wildly. "How do you expect me to rest, with my girlfriend killed and my mother—"

"I think you should *rest*," Con said more forcefully. "And no more calls. There are others who'd take a dimmer view of all this."

"A dimmer view of murder?" Joe echoed furiously. He raced up the stairs into the attic and froze.

Under the wan glow of the single electric light, the attic room was a lot less shadowy. There was the usual bric-a-brac, a few ancient trunks, and the rocking chair, thick with dust.

But there was no trace of blood, a knife . . . or Joe's mother.

Chapter

8

"THIS IS CRAZY," Joe Hardy muttered, staring around in shock. For a second he had the irrational idea of peeking under some of the piled-up family keepsakes, as if he could uncover his mother's body that way.

Joe shook his head. That would make about as much sense as accusing Con Riley and his partner, who had just entered the attic again, of spiriting Mrs. Hardy out the window.

"She was right there," Joe said, pointing to the chair. His voice sounded lame, even to his own ears.

"Judging from the dust on the seat, I'd say that chair hasn't been disturbed for months," Officer Horvath said. "Ever since that equally dusty box of Christmas lights was leaned up against it."

Joe bridled at the young policeman's snide tone. But he held back an angry answer as he looked at the box of lights. It leaned up against the back of the rocking chair, and it *was* just as dusty as the seat. Nobody could have sat in the chair without dislodging that box. Yet they were both there, dusty and apparently untouched.

"But I saw—" Then Joe shut up. Why sound even more stupid than he did now?

"You've been under a lot of pressure," Con Riley said, in the sort of low, soothing voice people usually save for crying children or dangerous maniacs. "I couldn't say what you saw up here, but it's pretty obvious what we're seeing now. It's not a police matter."

Yet Joe caught the unspoken part of what Con was saying. If I keep making trouble, Joe thought, they'll start calling for straitjackets.

"I just don't understand it," Joe said.

"Maybe you'll understand tomorrow, after a good night's sleep and when you're feeling calmer. I'll check in with you then."

In other words, Joe thought, Don't call us, we'll call you. Otherwise, I get a whole new reputation, as the wacko Hardy brother.

Joe said very little as he showed the two police officers to the door. Officer Riley had little to say, either, except for another suggestion that Joe take it easy.

Feeling helpless, Joe watched the patrol car head down Elm Street. The police wouldn't listen to him now, not even Con. Joe went back into the brightly lit house. He threw himself down on the living room couch to try to sort things out.

He thought about calling his father in New York. But what could he say? That he had seen his mother with a dagger in her chest, but now her body and all evidence of a murder had disappeared? Could he have imagined the whole scene he'd discovered upstairs?

Sure, if he'd suddenly gone out of his mind. Or maybe it had been just a very detailed dream—a nightmare. But he'd been up and around, unless he'd been sleepwalking. That just didn't seem to hold together as a theory.

Joe sighed. Maybe if Frank were here, he'd come up with some brilliant piece of psychology to explain everything. And he'd know whether they should call their father or wait. He suddenly missed his brother.

The phone rang, startling Joe. He picked it up and said hello.

"Joe, Phil Cohen here."

Joe relaxed a little at the sound of his friend's voice. "How's it going?"

"I'm having an interesting time in my lab with that candle you gave me," Phil said.

"Well, then, you're ahead of the police lab," Joe told him.

"They'll be interested when they get into it. According to my tests, some mighty nasty chemicals were mixed in that wax." Phil's voice took on a note of warning. "You'd better take it easy. There were hallucinogens in the wax."

"You mean I might see things?" Joe said slowly.

"It's possible. If I were you, I'd stick around the house for the rest of the evening."

"Thanks, Phil, I appreciate that. And I promise, I'll take it easy." Frowning, Joe hung up the phone.

Could this explain the nightmarish scene he'd come upon upstairs?

At least, Joe thought, he'd have something to talk about with Con Riley the next day. That would be a good thing. It would be hard to be taken seriously as a detective if he got a reputation for seeing things that weren't there.

Sighing, Joe rubbed his aching head. He closed his eyes. . . .

The ringing of the phone brought him awake. Joe stared around fuzzily. Whatever they put in those candles certainly knocked the stuffing out of me, he thought.

He fumbled the phone off the hook. "Hello?"

He heard a familiar voice on the line, an impossible but familiar voice. "It's midnight, Joe," Iola said, "the witching hour. You don't listen, darling. I warned you that the dead had come for the living. You could have come quietly, but you didn't. So, we've taken two for one. First Vanessa, then your mother."

The hairs on the back of Joe's neck began to prickle. How could they know about his mother if his vision of her dead body had been a hallucination?

And where *was* his mother, anyway?

"But it's you I want," Iola said in a chilling voice. "I've always wanted you."

"I don't know what you want or who you are," Joe shouted angrily into the phone. "But if you think you're going to play with my head, you're wrong."

"I just told you what I want," Iola said, a mocking tone in her voice. "I want you. But I always had competition, didn't I? Like that blond girl you were hitting on right before I was killed. What was her name? Val?"

Joe stood in silence, partly from amazement, partly from guilt. He *had* been flirting with another girl the day Iola died. But how could this voice know about that?

Unless, of course, this was the real Iola.

She continued the whole horrible story. "We were giving out leaflets at the Bayport Mall that day, and the last supply was in your car. I came to ask for help and found you with that girl. Do you remember what you did?"

Joe didn't answer.

"You said you'd be with me in a minute and just played with your car keys."

How did she know? How?

"You made a fool of me in front of that girl, so I grabbed the keys and went off to your car by myself. And you know what happened then, Joe. I set off a bomb meant for you."

"Iola," Joe said in a hoarse voice.

"What are you going to say? That you're sorry? It's a little too late for that, Joe. Of course, I see you have a new blond now. At least you *had* one this afternoon."

Joe snapped out of his stunned silence. "I don't care who or what you are," he said hotly into the phone. "If you had business with me, *I'm* the one you should have come to."

"No," the voice of Iola said. "You're the one I'm coming *for*. Soon we'll be together again, Joe. Forever."

There was a click, and Joe heard the hum of the dial tone.

His hope that his troubles were all hallucinations had just been destroyed. And unless he was ready to believe in ghosts, he didn't have a clue as to what was going on.

"This is crazy," Frank Hardy said, staring around in disbelief at the torture chamber. The local sheriff stood behind him with deputies plus a contingent of state troopers.

The only problem was, they'd found absolutely nothing.

The old madhouse was still there, but Callie's body was gone. So were the net that had entrapped Frank, the swinging blade, and the big table.

Frank had led the sheriff and state troopers to the room he considered a torture chamber. But when they got there, Frank and the lawmen found only a large, empty echoing room.

In disbelief, Frank stood in the hallway, turning his flashlight left, then right. No. This was the door, this was the room.

"It was right in here," Frank said. "A heavy table, with my girlfriend strapped down, and a blade that came down from the ceiling."

"I read that story, too," the local sheriff said. He had not been happy about being dragged away from home. And judging from the look the law officer gave the state patrol, Frank realized the sheriff probably felt he was being made a fool of by some punk kid. "Freshman year in high school, that's when I read it. Thought it was farfetched back then. Even sillier today."

He knelt in the doorway and ran a finger through the layer of thick dust that lay on the floor. "You say you came in here, didn't you? Well, how did you do that? By floating in mid-air? I guess that's it, since you left no footprints on the floor."

Frank stared in dismay at the unbroken carpet of dust that covered the stone floor of the room. The dust seemed just as thick where the table had been as it was everywhere else on the untouched floor.

The sheriff was right. Except for some small scrape marks from the door, the dust hadn't been disturbed.

"Next time you make up a story, son, at least *try* to back it up a little." The sheriff shook his head in disgust.

"Look, I'm telling you what I saw. You can check my story out. I arrived here this evening by chartered plane with my girlfriend. And now she's disappeared."

"Then in seventy-two hours you can declare her a missing person," the sheriff broke in. "Till then, I'm not wasting time on some fool Halloween stunt." He looked at his watch. "It's after eleven o'clock. What I suggest is that you take a motel room back in town, Mr. Hardy. In fact, take *two* rooms, in case the young lady, uh, turns up. I've had enough of this."

On the drive back to town, Frank's rented car was wedged in the middle of the procession of law vehicles. The whole parade stopped at a motel on the edge of town, and the sheriff got out and booked two rooms. "My advice is to stay here and stay out of trouble," he said to Frank.

But as soon as the police vehicles were gone, Frank was back in his car, heading for the Lazarus Clinic. He was back by midnight.

The old, heavy door was still ajar as Frank headed up the drive, his footsteps crunching on the gravel. The inside still looked the same as he wandered the halls, swinging his flashlight from side to side.

But the place wasn't quiet. Ahead of him, Frank heard scuffling noises. Footsteps—he was sure of it.

At the end of a corridor and around the corner, he suddenly heard a voice. "Frank!"

That was Callie! "Frank! Watch out—"

The voice was suddenly cut off, but Frank was already running down the hall. He turned the corner to find another corridor, also empty.

Frank whirled at the sound of rusty hinges screeching behind him. One of the doors he'd passed swung open, and a man stepped out. He was tall and dark haired, with a long, thin, expressionless face. Frank had known him first as Detective Inspector Sam Butler of the Bayport Police. Then he'd known him as Al-Rousasa, one of the top terrorists working for the Assassins.

This is impossible! Frank thought. I saw Al-Rousasa die. Unless . . .

The Assassin reached under his short leather jacket and pulled out an automatic pistol. Frank dodged around the corner. Halloween, he thought, when the dead walk.

He found himself in a shorter corridor, with

three branches leading into it. He could hear footsteps in two of these hallways. The footsteps were growing louder, closer.

Frank broke into a sweat. He felt surrounded by invisible adversaries. His heart pounding rapidly, he started down the only hall that was silent. He turned out his flashlight, unwilling to give anyone a target. Behind him he could hear the sounds of his pursuers. They seemed to be growing in number. Where were they when I was here with the police? Frank wondered.

He was beginning to feel seriously outnumbered when he found himself stumbling into a chapel, its tall, narrow windows smashed out. Waning moonlight poured in on sagging wooden benches. The glow also illuminated a man of average height, undistinguished features, and graying hair, wearing a rumpled trench coat and standing near the altar.

It was the Hardys' Network contact, the Gray Man.

Frank stopped in the center aisle of the chapel to catch his breath. The Gray Man had never been one of Frank's favorite people, but at that moment he was filled with relief to see the tall, serious-looking man. "You came up early after all!" Frank exclaimed. "Am I glad to see you. There's a whole bunch of terrorist types chasing me."

Without speaking, the government agent

reached into his coat pocket and pulled out a pistol.

"I think we'll need more than that to handle them," Frank said. "Do you have more agents in the vicinity?"

The Gray Man didn't say a word. He raised the gun, aimed it at Frank, and fired.

Chapter

9

THE ROAR of the gunshot was deafening, and the muzzle flash was blinding.

But the bullet went over Frank Hardy's head. The instant he saw the gun swinging his way, he threw himself to the floor. Then he scrambled up and ducked behind one of the benches as the Gray Man sent a second shot, then a third one his way.

Bullets tore through the wood of the old pews. "You might as well give up, Hardy," said the Gray Man. "Vanessa Bender, Callie Shaw, and by dawn your brother. Our plans are set. There is no way out for you."

As soon as Frank heard the voice, he paused in his crouching progress. That wasn't the Gray Man speaking! The intelligence agent had a distinctive voice, and Frank always recognized it. A chill passed through Frank's body as he realized that the Assassins had created a clone of the government agent.

Frank had come to the Lazarus Clinic looking for doubles. Now he realized he'd found much more than he'd bargained for—the clone of the late Al-Rousasa and one of the Gray Man. Of course, this discovery wouldn't mean much if he got killed in the next few minutes. He had to get past this phony Gray Man and out one of the chapel windows. And he had to do it immediately. He could hear voices in the corridor behind him.

Holding his breath, Frank took his flashlight and tossed it across the chapel aisle toward the other pews. The flashlight clattered along one pew, and Frank heard bullets splintering the wood as the Gray Man fired in the direction of the sound.

Then Frank rose, picking up the long wooden bench as he stood up. Straining every muscle, he lifted the pew and hurled it at the gunman.

The phony agent had been aiming in the wrong direction. Now as he turned the gun on Frank, the pew smashed into him, knocking him flat.

Frank broke into motion, dashing across the floor and diving out one of the broken windows. And not a moment too soon, he thought. He heard a roar of angry voices in the chapel. His pursuers had arrived.

Frank zigzagged across a garden overgrown with weeds and brambles. He was on the opposite end of the complex from the spot where he'd left his car. Doubling back was out of the question. Turning briefly, he saw a group of men—eight to ten, he guessed—coming out of the chapel.

Ahead was a cyclone fence and beyond that, forest. Frank ducked behind a row of bushes, then ran for the barrier. Fierce Maine winters and spring thaws had undermined several of the fence posts, causing the wire mesh to sag deeply. In one place the fence was almost down, and Frank scrambled over it.

Behind him, he heard a cry. He had been spotted, he thought, not daring to look back. The chase was on.

Running through a forest with only moonlight to guide him and no weapon bigger than a pocketknife was not Frank Hardy's idea of fun. Unseen branches whipped at his face, and he could make out the tree trunks only as darker portions of shadow among the other shadows. Frank was running so fast that he didn't discover the ten-foot-deep gully until he went tumbling down into it. By the time he scrambled up the other side, he was battered and bruised, his clothes were torn, and his flashlight was gone.

Behind him, he could see the little glowing spots of light that indicated his pursuers' positions.

So long as they keep those flashlights on, I've got a chance, Frank thought. At least I'll know where they are.

The terrorists behind him assumed the usual hunting formation. Whether it's a deer or a man, the system is the same, Frank thought.

From the positions of the flashlights' beams, he could tell that most of the pursuers had joined together in a skirmish line, heading straight into the woods. They were supposed to drive him forward, herding him. The men on the edges of the line would push faster into the forest, trying to cut off his retreat. In the end, the wing men would meet as the line became a circle. Then they'd close in to finish him.

Frank shivered at the thought. The problem was, he'd never outrun his pursuers while they had flashlights and he didn't.

Off to the side, he heard someone crashing through the underbrush and briefly saw the beam from a flashlight. If he could get that flashlight, Frank thought, he would have a fair chance of escaping his pursuers.

He dashed ahead of the skirmish line until he found a big oak, its leaves mostly shed, with bramble bushes close by. Frank scrambled up the trunk, picked a sturdy branch, and climbed out on it until he was over a bush. Reaching down, Frank grabbed one of the upper branches of the bush and shook it vigorously. Branches vibrated together and dead leaves fell, making enough noise to ensure his pursuer would head in that direction.

Frank gave another shake, and another. He saw the beam of the flashlight coming closer. Now Frank could make out the person behind it: the fake Gray Man, blundering through the forest in a trench coat. The man kept getting stuck on bushes, then having to free himself.

Frank tried one final shake of the bush. The light moved that way, and Frank froze. The untrained tracker kept his beam at ground level.

Frank waited until the imposter was almost directly under his branch. Then he jumped.

He landed on the man's shoulders, knocking him down into a pile of damp leaves. They slipped and spun for a couple of seconds, the Gray Man clone trying to get his gun into position. In the struggle, the flashlight rolled away.

Fighting by feel and with great good luck, Frank managed to land a blow to the side of his opponent's head. The double went limp.

Frank rose to his feet and looked for the flashlight. There it was, still throwing a beam, after having rolled under one of the nearby bramble branches. Frank held the long branch aside, and stooped down to reach for the flashlight with his other hand.

Just as his fingers closed on the metal tube, he heard movement. Frank turned to find the false Gray Man on his knees right behind him, gun in hand.

Frank ducked and let go of the thorny branch. It snapped back, right into the gunman's face. He screamed. Frank grabbed a rock, leapt on the man, and knocked him out.

"Josip!" a voice called out of the darkness. "What's wrong?"

"Thorns," Frank called back, hoping his Gray Man voice would sound convincing in a one-word answer.

He grinned. It was even the truth.

Frank picked up the flashlight and angled away from the hunters, falling farther and farther back as they moved to encircle the area where they supposed him to be. Soon enough Josip, the Gray Man double, was going to wake up. Before that happened, Frank knew he would have to disappear.

He gave himself another couple of minutes' traveling with the aid of the flashlight. Then he turned it off and, moving as quietly as he could, headed directly away from the area of the search. By going cross-country, he knew he had a decent chance of reaching the main highway that cut through that part of the state.

Frank found a track through the forest and set off at a jog. He hadn't gone very far when he heard yelling in the distance. Josip must have made his report, Frank thought. One man began shouting orders. Frank turned. The lights of the pursuers abruptly winked out.

Now Frank knew he wouldn't be able to tell where his pursuers were. But they couldn't see where they were going, either. If he heard rustling in the woods, he'd have to get away from it. If they heard rustling, they'd probably shoot. But they might be shooting one of their own people.

Frank found a clearing in the woods and stopped for a second to estimate his position from the moon. If he kept in this direction, he thought, he should come upon the highway.

He ran as fast as he could across the open space. He knew that if anybody came on him now, he'd make a wonderful target.

He safely reached the far side of the clearing and discovered that the track continued there. But it began to curve away from the direction Frank had to follow. He pushed off into the woods again, dodging into a stand of ancient pines. The darkness under the trees was profound, their interwoven boughs keeping out the moonlight. There were no brambles or blackberry bushes to blunder into, but to Frank's ears his rustling progress through the dried, fallen needles might as well have been a brass band announcing his position.

Pine needles gave way to a rocky hillside, and Frank scrambled down, doing his best to stay under cover. When he was hidden in the shadows of a small valley, he paused to glance back.

The moon's eerie orange radiance spotlit

several men as they began descending the rocks. They must have found the pathway, too, Frank thought.

He had no choice now but to climb up the other side of the valley. Knowing he would probably be seen, he started up the hilly area. Shouting behind him told him he'd been right—his pursuers had spotted him.

Looks like I've had it, he thought.

But as he reached the summit, he found himself overlooking the highway. He could see headlights moving along the winding road.

The highway seemed to have been cut through a hilly area, and the way down to the road was very steep. There was only one thing to do, Frank thought. In a rattle of loose rocks, he sent himself tobogganing down the slope toward the road. He flew along patches of bare rock, starting a little landslide of gravel. He knew that he had to keep himself from going into a tumble, or he was in danger of breaking an arm—or his neck.

Luckily, the slope evened out toward the bottom. Frank snatched at bushes and vines to stop his rate of descent. He rolled to an ungraceful stop right on the shoulder of the road.

He knew that his pursuers must have reached the hilltop by now. Would they risk the slide down? he wondered. Just then he saw the headlights of a light, open-bed truck, which was laboring up the gradient.

Frank took cover behind some roadside brush. As the headlights came past him, Frank darted out. He realized that, for a few seconds, he'd be silhouetted against the truck's taillights. If his pursuers had a real marksman at the top of the hill . . .

He leapt for the rear of the truck.

Made it! The moon disappeared behind the hills, and the truck rolled onward.

When it pulled into a rest stop, Frank hopped off. He went into the diner, dug through his pockets for change, and called home. There was no answer.

This is bad, Frank thought. Joe is in danger, and I can't warn him about what's going on. He had turned from the phone in despair when a bearded, cheerful-looking man stopped on the way back from the rest room.

"Goshamighty," the man said, staring at Frank. "You been out wrestling bears, son?"

Frank looked down at his torn and dirty clothing. "Something like that," Frank said.

The man shook his head. "You look like you could use some help."

"My problem is that I have to get to the local airport," Frank said. "I have a plane waiting there for me."

The man grinned. "Well, it sounds like times have changed since my days on the road. You sure you don't need some money?"

"Thanks," Frank said. "All I need is a lift to the airport."

Still smiling, the man said, "Come on, then," and walked outside to his car. Frank was grateful that the man asked no questions as he drove. They arrived at the airport to find the plane Frank had chartered in Bayport all gassed up and ready to go, just as he'd arranged on landing.

Frank would always remember the man's dumbfounded look when they rolled out the plane.

After thanking the stranger, Frank got into the plane. He noticed that the man was still standing there, watching. Frank waved. Poor man probably thinks I'm a high-tech hobo or a very weird millionaire.

Once he was in the air, Frank groaned. It was almost half past one. He was tired, and now he had the leisure to feel his bruises. And since he wasn't running for his life, he had time to think about the terrible events at the Lazarus Clinic. Obviously the clone makers were back at work. But why had they made a clone of the Gray Man? Were the Assassins planning on infiltrating the Network?

It was definitely a possibility, Frank thought. Their double of the Gray Man could even give false testimony at the trial. Frank had a sinking feeling in the pit of his stomach. The real Network agent might be out of the game permanently. Had the man he talked with on the phone earlier been the real thing or the Assassin copy, luring him up to the Lazarus Clinic? Frank didn't know.

He did know one thing, however. The Assassins had killed Vanessa Bender and Callie Shaw.

Frank looked out the cockpit at the starlit sky, forcing back the emotions that threatened to overwhelm him.

I promise you this, Callie, he vowed silently. Whoever killed you, I'll get them. I'll make them pay.

Whatever it takes.

Chapter

10

"YOU'RE THE ONE I'm coming for." The telephone threat kept echoing in Joe Hardy's head. Ghost, clone, or just a figment of Joe's imagination, Iola had certainly turned out to be real enough.

Joe fell back against the couch cushions.

If it's me she wants, why doesn't she come and get me? Why did she have to take Vanessa?

Joe's eyes closed in pain. Why did she have to take his mother?

He fought hard to make some sense of the nightmare that entrapped him. But the answers kept evading him. If only there was something physical he could fight, wrestle with, Joe knew he could handle it. But he felt as if he were fighting fog.

He didn't even know if his enemy existed. Suppose the Iola who was torturing him was a product of the devilish clone techniques developed at the Lazarus Clinic. Then he supposed he should try for a confrontation, hoping for a chance to grab her and learn the truth.

And if he couldn't catch her, would that mean he really was dealing with a ghost? A vengeful spirit out to punish him?

Joe rubbed his aching head. The fumes from those candles must still be affecting me, he thought. He hoped Frank was in a better state. Of course, Callie had dragged Frank out first.

I got the longer dose, Joe thought.

Joe pushed himself up from the couch, then walked to the large bay window. Outside, the night was quiet. The only movement he could see on the street was the swirling of dead leaves. Overhead, thin clouds scudded across the huge orange face of the moon.

Joe stared out the window as images of death flashed before his eyes: an exploding car, a boat in flames, a gold dagger hilt ringed by a circle of crimson.

Cold determination began to grow within him. Frank's not around to help, so it's all up to me, he told himself.

Something struck the window with a wet, mushy sound.

Joe hadn't seen anyone, but it was obvious

that the older kids were still out playing Halloween pranks. He felt a stab of anger. Well, this was the wrong house to play a trick on tonight.

He dashed to the door and flung it open, hoping to catch the culprit, but the street was empty. There were no running footsteps, no sound of a car driving off, no one hiding behind a tree. He glanced around, bewildered.

Joe walked outside to check the window. As he came closer, he smelled something brackish. He looked at the window, then down at the ground. The prankster had thrown a bundle of seaweed. That was a strange Halloween prank, Joe thought.

The seaweed triggered thoughts of the events that afternoon at the dock. More than nine hours had passed since the explosion. The police had had their chance to go over the docks and the wreckage. If they had found anything suspicious, they would have called him. It was obvious they had turned up nothing.

"Now it's my turn." Joe ducked back inside to grab his jacket.

He glanced at the phone and wished he could contact Frank, just to be sure he was all right.

But that wasn't possible, and time was not on his side.

The marina dock was deserted when Joe pulled up in the van. All types of boats were anchored there, bobbing and swaying in the ebbing tide. The rigging of the sailboats creaked and moaned.

Joe reached into the glove compartment and pulled out a flashlight. He got out of the van, took a deep breath, and started down the pier, toward the area where the explosion had occurred.

A cold, stiff breeze seemed to swell as Joe neared the site of Vanessa's death.

Police tape stretched from a mooring post on one side to a small equipment shed on the other. It blocked off the end of the pier—or what was left of it. Most of the wharf's planking was either charred, splintered, or completely blown away. Joe slipped under the tape and cautiously moved along the damaged area. Several boards creaked and shifted under his weight.

"This is not a good idea," he muttered, as he stepped back a bit.

He flicked the flashlight's switch and began searching the area. For a while his effort seemed futile. Then suddenly the light reflected off something small but shiny. The object was caught up in some discarded fishing net thrown in a heap next to one of the posts.

"Vanessa's pin!" Joe exclaimed. He scooped up the small piece of jewelry, a handmade pin in the shape of a comical cat's face. The pin had always reminded Joe of a cartoon he used to watch on TV as a child. "What's it doing here?" he wondered.

Could it have been blown here when she— Joe squeezed his eyes shut, trying to block out the thought.

He went back to the police line and began a methodical, inch-by-inch search of the pier. He reached the spot where he'd found the pin and continued to move, shining his flashlight in careful sweeps, his eyes straining for something that might give him a clue to the explosion.

The image of Vanessa waving to him from the boat flashed in his mind. Again Joe tried to push it away.

He was nearly to the end of the damaged pier when he heard the sound. It was soft at first, barely a whisper. Then it grew louder. It was the sound of tortured breathing, of someone gasping for air.

Joe rushed forward, feeling the weakened structure shift beneath his feet. He looked toward the water, and suddenly his own lungs seemed to be paralyzed. His flashlight dropped from nerveless fingers and rolled into the water below.

There before him was Vanessa, rising from the water, her hair dripping wet, her expression frightened but recognizable. Seaweed was draped about her shoulders like a shroud.

Vanessa ascended until she stood, barely knee deep, in water Joe knew to be at least ten feet deep. She stared up at him with accusing eyes, her pale face almost luminescent.

"Vanessa?" Joe stammered. "Y-y-you didn't—"

"No, I'm dead all right," the girl said. Her voice sounded strange, garbled, as if it were bubbling up from under water. "But the explosion didn't kill me, Joe. It was the water. I drowned. Why didn't you try to save me? Why did you let me die, Joe?"

Joe took a step forward, his hands out, pleading. "I *tried* to reach you, but they wouldn't let me."

"You killed me!" Vanessa's hands flew upward, and suddenly Joe felt the dock breaking up beneath him.

"Join me, Joe! Join us!"

The boards made a sickening crack, and the pier where Joe was standing gave way. He turned and took a flying leap. He managed to land facedown on another section of the pier. He grabbed on to a charred beam. Razorlike wooden splinters stabbed into his left palm, sending ribbons of pain through his hand.

Joe didn't dare let go. He could feel this part of the pier giving way, too. He forced himself to move forward on his stomach. He grabbed another plank of the pier. He could see now that the burned wood had split, and he could feel it sagging dangerously under his weight. Soon it would break completely, dumping him into the rubble-filled water below.

Joe quickly scrambled toward the undamaged part of the pier. Not a moment too soon, he thought as he heard the boards behind him hitting the water with a thundering sound.

Breathing heavily, Joe stood up and turned back toward the water.

Vanessa was gone.

In the moonlight Joe stared at the water's surface, desperately searching for ripples, air bubbles—*anything* sane to explain the irrational event that had just happened.

Then he dropped to his knees and put his face in his hands. "It's not possible," he muttered. "None of this stuff is possible." Maybe he was going nuts, he thought.

He had no idea how much time passed before he stood and made his way back to the van. He didn't look at the water again, but he couldn't help thinking, I didn't mean to hurt you, Vanessa. I didn't want it to end this way.

There was nowhere to rest from the nightmare.

Joe was back home, in the middle of bandaging his injured hand after taking out the splinters, when the phone began ringing.

What if it was Iola again? Joe thought, his heart pounding rapidly. He stared at the phone, letting six rings go by.

Then the thought that it might be Frank

flashed through his mind. He grabbed the receiver.

"Where have you been?" It was Chet Morton, and Joe heard the agitation in his friend's voice. "I've been calling all night and either getting busy signals or no answer."

Joe looked at his watch. It was one in the morning. "Well, you sure are persistent."

"I had to make sure you were okay," Chet said. "After what Con Riley told me—"

"What did Con say? That I need a keeper?"

Chet didn't answer the question. He simply said, "Just stay put. I want to see you."

About half an hour later, the doorbell rang, and there was Chet.

"Hey, buddy." Chet Morton stood in the doorway, looking a little embarrassed and uncomfortable about his late-night visit. "Can I come in?"

"Sure," Joe said eagerly. After thinking about it, he'd decided it would be good to have a friend to talk to. Chet might be able to help him sort things out.

"I wanted to see for myself how you were doing," Chet said as he stepped inside. There was concern in his voice. "Con Riley told me what happened earlier tonight. He said you seemed confused." Chet fumbled for words. "Con thought you shouldn't be—"

"Alone?" Joe snapped, hurling himself onto the living room couch. "Does he think I'm going to hurt myself?"

Chet looked down at the bandage Joe had awkwardly wrapped around his hand. "How'd that happen?"

"I was at the docks and—" Joe stopped himself. What was he going to say? That he nearly fell through the pier chasing a ghost?

"You were there to look for something? Clues?" Chet asked.

Joe nodded.

"Find anything?"

Joe hesitated. "No," he said finally.

"You need rest, Joe. You need to put all of this on hold till you're thinking more clearly."

Joe threw up his hands. "How can I?" he demanded. "Vanessa gets blown to bits, and my mother is murdered in our own house! How can I sit still after that?"

"Con told me what you saw," Chet said slowly, "or what you think you saw. But there's no evidence of a murder."

"I saw the *body*, Chet!"

"Then where is it now?" Chet asked gently.

Joe turned away from the worry and disbelief he saw in his friend's face. "I don't know."

"Look, I know how you feel."

"You don't have a clue!" Joe shouted, whipping around to face Chet. "You haven't lost a mother and a girlfriend!"

Chet cut Joe off, his eyes burning. "I lost a sister."

"And I bet you blame me for that, don't you?"

"Not anymore." Chet's face fell the moment he said it. "Now isn't the time to be saying this."

"No. I've got to know. You *did* blame me?" Joe asked.

Chet lowered his head for a moment. "When Iola died, I thought, Why did *she* have to be the one? Why did *she* have to go to the car? If she hadn't been with you . . ." His voice trailed off.

Joe was silent.

"I had to blame someone," Chet said at last. "But after a while I realized I was wrong."

"No, Chet. You were right." Joe's voice was hoarse. "If Iola hadn't been with me, she'd still be alive. The same goes for Vanessa. Even Mom."

Joe looked up with haunted eyes. "Do you think *they* blame me, Chet?"

"Joe, that's not what I meant."

"Go home, Chet." Joe suddenly rose and led his friend back to the door. "Go home before someone gets you, too."

Chet only looked more concerned. He tried to put a hand on Joe's shoulder, but the younger Hardy moved away from him. "Promise me you're not going to do anything stupid," Chet said.

"I promise."

"You know where I am. Call me anytime," Chet said as Joe saw him out the door.

"Sure. And thanks, Chet." Joe closed the door. Absently he reached into his jeans pocket and pulled out Vanessa's cat pin. So many people had died because they got close to him, he thought, staring at the pin.

His thoughts were interrupted when the doorbell rang again.

Assuming that Chet had returned, Joe opened the door. A child stood there, dressed in a black hooded robe and wearing a skull mask.

Joe frowned at the child. "Trick-or-treat time is over," he said sternly. "Your folks must be worried sick about you. You should get home."

Instead of holding out a treat bag, the masked child held out a piece of paper. "Got this for you." His voice sounded strange through the rubber mask.

Joe's frown deepened as he looked suspiciously at the folded paper. "What is this, some stupid prank?"

"A lady gave me this to give you," the child said. He pushed the note at Joe. "Here."

Joe unfolded the paper and read a message scrawled in red ink.

"The grave's a fine and private place,
But none, I think, do there embrace."

My rest is lonely, Joe. Come to me, or else another will join me.

The kid had edged back while Joe was reading. Now he leapt away as Joe grabbed for him. "Who gave you this?" Joe demanded.

"Her," the child replied, pointing up the street toward a lamppost.

In the circle of light stood the same figure Joe had seen outside the police station.

The wind blew her dark hair. The light seemed to sink into her marble white skin.

Iola gave him a ghastly grin, then faded back into the shadows.

Chapter

11

JOE BOLTED FROM the front porch and ran to the corner. He hoped he'd hear some sound— the roar of a car's engine, the slap of running feet—to show that the girl who'd stood there was flesh and blood.

But he heard and saw nothing. It was as if Iola had turned to mist and disappeared.

Joe rubbed a trembling hand across his eyes. "Maybe I *am* going nuts," he muttered. "Or maybe there are such things as ghosts."

If such things as vengeful spirits did stalk the night, what better time than Halloween for them to walk the earth?

"She's playing with me," Joe whispered. "She doesn't just want revenge, she wants me to suffer." He ran into the house, grabbed his jacket and car keys, then dashed back out and jumped into the van.

" 'The grave's a fine and private place,' " he quoted, gunning the engine. "Well, I'm in the mood to crash your private party." Joe's voice rose, even though there was no one for him to talk to. "You want me? Fine! I'm coming, Iola. And all this ends tonight, one way or another!"

The Cessna had barely rolled to a stop in front of the hangar when Frank jumped down from the cockpit. For the whole trip back to Bayport, he'd pressed every ounce of power out of the twin engines. A tail wind had helped get him back in less than two hours. Frank yawned and stretched. He'd be glad to get home.

"Hold on there," came a gruff voice. Frank turned to see Matt, Rick Meyerhold's mechanic, approaching the plane. The tall, lanky, gray-haired man took care of the flight school's small fleet of planes as if they were his children.

The mechanic regarded Frank's disheveled appearance. "Hope the plane came back better than you did," he said grumpily. "Heard about this big fight here. Doctor made Mr. M. go to bed, so I figured I'd wait till you came back."

"Is Rick going to be all right?" Frank asked.

Matt shrugged. "Just a little shook up. But if I know Mr. M., he'll probably be running classes tomorrow." He jerked a thumb back at the hangar. "What were you doing in there, playing catch? There were boxes all over the place."

"We probably should have stayed to clean things up, but we were in a hurry."

"You and your young lady friend," Matt said. He cocked his head and looked over at the plane. "Where is she now?"

"She stayed in Maine," Frank said quietly, grief fighting with exhaustion.

"Well," Matt said, reaching into his back pocket and pulling out a scarf, "I found this on the hangar floor. Do you know if it's hers?"

Frank took it gently. "Yeah, that's hers. I must have dropped it during the fight. Thanks."

Matt wished him a good night. "Or rather, good morning," the mechanic said with a grin.

Tucking the scarf in his jacket pocket, Frank ran across the field and into the terminal. He quickly found a pay phone and dialed home.

"Come on, Joe, pick up the phone." But his brother didn't answer. Frank slammed down the receiver and headed straight for the parking lot.

Callie's car was right where they had left it only a few hours before. Frank reached under the front bumper and removed a little box attached there by magnets. Inside was a spare set of car keys. Frank smiled sadly. Callie was so afraid she'd lose her keys somewhere, she'd ordered the box from a catalog.

Frank felt his eyes begin to sting. No time for tears now, he thought. He had to get home and make sure Joe was all right. Then he would have to do the hardest thing he'd ever had to do in his life. He would have to call Callie's parents.

Frank opened the door, got behind the wheel, and threw the car into gear. The tires screeched on the pavement as he sped out of the lot.

This place sure looks private, Joe Hardy thought as he pulled up at the gates to Bayport's cemetery. It was located at the edge of town in an area sparsely inhabited—at least by the living, Joe thought.

He climbed over the low stone wall surrounding the cemetery, then headed down a gravel path under the starlight. The cold cut through him, and Joe trembled inside and out. But he kept moving toward the Morton mausoleum.

Mist was rising from the ground as Joe finally reached his destination. The small stone structure rested at the foot of a hill just past a grove of pine trees. Once Iola had pointed it out to him, and Frank and Joe could never have imagined that all too soon Iola's closed coffin would be placed there. Joe's heart ached at the memory. The coffin had been a symbol, in a way, of her death, for as with Vanessa, the explosion hadn't left a trace of her to bury.

A sickly glow seemed to light the mist as Joe moved toward the mausoleum. Joe expected the metal door of the mausoleum to be locked, but it swung easily inward at the pressure of his hand.

Total darkness and chilly, musty air greeted him. There was complete silence. Even the wind seemed to have died away. Joe took a step forward, and the blackness instantly erupted.

He heard screeching and the sound of flapping wings. Fluttering furry shapes flashed past his face, sometimes actually brushing it.

Joe threw his arms up to protect himself against the wave of bats. As he did so, he heard a woman's laughter echoing off the walls of the mausoleum, almost blending with the high-pitched call of the bats.

Then Joe felt a sharp pain at his neck. Liquid fire raced through his veins.

"Join us," the woman cried out.

In that moment Joe's world shattered. To his unbelieving eyes, the small stone structure he stood in seemed to shift and grow.

He stumbled outside. The odd glow he'd noticed earlier heightened. The bats around him filled the sky, shaping into a massive creature with wings and burning yellow eyes. This can't be happening, Joe told himself. But it was real!

Iola stood before him, pale as death. She seemed to be laughing at him.

Joe felt the ground crack beneath his feet. Tombstones fell and exploded. And from the earth the dead rose. Rank and decayed, they oozed from their graves, advancing on Joe Hardy.

Chapter

12

DEATH WAS haunting Elm Street. As he parked in front of his house, Frank Hardy caught a glimpse of a little skull-face peering at him from some low bushes.

He took a step in that direction, and a short, robed figure burst onto the sidewalk, a trick-or-treat bag rattling as it ran.

What was a little kid doing out at nearly four in the morning? Frank wondered. But he had other things to worry about. The Hardy house gleamed like a beacon on the otherwise dark street. Every light was on.

Frank had found that a welcome sight when he pulled up, thinking that Joe and his mother might be waiting up for him.

Then he noticed the door was ajar. After a quick search of the house, both upstairs and down, Frank realized he was very much alone.

"Where are you two?" he said urgently. Judging by the hour, Frank was fairly certain neither Joe nor his mother was visiting friends.

Frank took a deep breath, fighting his fatigue and concern, then went to check out the garage. It was the only place he hadn't looked. The garage was empty. He vaguely remembered that his mother had left the car at the airport for his dad and aunt Gertrude. Frank stood in the middle of the garage, trying to make sense of the bizarre events of this night.

The attempts on our lives suggest a revenge plot, Frank reasoned. But by whom?

He recalled the attack at the airport earlier, the cross-country chase by the Lazarus clones. Then came the vision he least wanted. He saw Callie, bound and gagged, her eyes wide above the scarf as he fought the net. The blade dropped, the blood, his screams . . .

Frank squeezed his eyes shut. There seemed to be an empty space in his chest where his heart should be. The action of the chase and the distraction of flying had held this feeling of desolation at bay. Now he was feeling the loss of his love full force. "Callie," he whispered.

Then fury washed over him. He rammed a fist into a wall of the garage.

Why? Why her, not me?

What were the Assassins doing? These guys were pros, with resources most nations would envy. They wouldn't kill just for the fun of it. There had to be a reason behind every bizarre murder. Frank took a deep breath, then slowly walked back into the house.

Revenge was certainly a powerful emotion, he thought. It could be the motive behind all of this, but it wouldn't explain everything he'd seen. The clone of the Gray Man seemed to indicate an attempt to infiltrate the Network. But why make a double of Al-Rousasa, a dead Assassin?

A chill ran through Frank. And why create another clone of the also-dead Iola Morton?

Frank hurried back to the house, worry eating at him. He'd seen how Joe had reacted to the phone call from Iola. Hearing his dead girlfriend's voice especially just after losing Vanessa . . .

He froze in the doorway. Psy-war. Psychological warfare. Someone was attacking Joe's mind—both of their minds. And suddenly Frank knew why.

"The trial," he whispered. "The United States *versus* an Assassin named Boris—or Brubaker. They want to stop our testimony."

Killing them wouldn't be enough. The Hardys had both given depositions and testified before the grand jury. Even if they were killed, their sworn statements could be used as evidence. But if they were discredited—shown to be acting irrationally . . . Frank wondered how his apparent antics that night would be described by the Maine sheriff or the highway patrol.

What had they been doing to Joe?

Just then Frank spotted a crumpled sheet of paper on the floor by the front door.

He wondered how he had missed it until he saw it was marked with his sneaker print. As he picked it up he noticed sticky stains on the paper.

His eyes narrowed. "Candy," he mused. Frank quickly glanced to the side of the door. His mother had gone out to buy trick-or-treat supplies, and she was always more than generous with the goodies. An overflowing bowl would be set up by the door, and there were always enough leftovers to keep Joe in candy for the next week.

But there wasn't any candy in sight.

That means she never came back from the store, Frank realized. Did Joe go looking for her?

Unfolding the note, he read the mocking message that had sent Joe racing from the house.

Key words stabbed at Frank's brain, plaguing him with doubt and fear. "The grave's a . . . private place . . ."

The cemetery. Didn't the Mortons have a mausoleum there?

Then Frank read the last line. "Come to me, or else another will join me."

Frank raced from the house and jumped into Callie's car. The cemetery where Iola was buried had to be a twenty-minute drive, normally. But this late at night, Frank felt certain he could make it in ten.

As he sped through the desolate streets, he couldn't help but worry. How long ago had the note arrived? Had Joe already gone to the cemetery and had he fallen into some kind of trap?

The question that worried Frank most was, Who else had been taken? The note implied that someone else would die. Was it referring to Callie? Frank's hands tightened on the steering wheel. Or had the Assassins taken their mother?

Frank floored the gas pedal, and the houses and trees whipped past in a blur. He needed to find some answers before his imagination took him over the edge into madness.

The Hardy van was easy to recognize as Frank parked at the cemetery gates. Frank left Callie's car, leapt over the stone wall, and proceeded down the gravel path. Now, where was the mausoleum? He remembered Iola pointing it out to them once. He remembered it was set close to a hill, near some pines. It was large enough that, even at night, it shouldn't be too hard to find.

The wind picked up, blowing leaves through

the air in whirling waves around Frank. He found his way by starlight. Suddenly a chittering swarm of bats passed overhead. Frank glanced up nervously. He had never seen so many bats before. A natural occurrence, he wondered, or some type of omen?

Picking up his pace, Frank hurried on. He spotted the pine trees and saw the outline of the mausoleum. But as he reached the trees, Frank heard a horrible sound, like the howl of a tortured animal.

He peered between two trees and gasped at the sight that confronted him.

The little hollow at the base of the hill was filled with wispy mist glowing with phosphorescent light as it twisted and curled into strange shapes. Standing in the middle, flailing and screaming in a frenzy, was Joe. As Frank watched, his brother sliced and smashed at the mist with a large shovel as though he were fighting demons. His eyes were wild with panic.

"Joe!" Frank rushed toward his brother.

At first Joe didn't seem to see him. Then he stopped, panting as Frank approached.

"Take it easy, Joe. It's just me."

Joe's eyes were glassy and staring.

"Whatever they did to you, we can fix it," Frank said in a soothing voice.

"You, too?" Joe Hardy's voice was almost a whimper. "They got you, too?"

"Who?" Frank asked.

"Them!" Joe screamed, waving toward the enveloping mist around them. Then he rushed at Frank, his shovel held high. "They got you," Joe bellowed. "But you won't get me!"

He swung the shovel in a killing blow, aimed right at Frank's head.

Chapter

13

JOE HARDY swung the shovel as if it were a baseball bat. But Frank knew the result would not be a home run. If the sharp metal head caught him in the neck, it could decapitate him.

Frank flung himself backward. The head of the shovel passed close enough to his face for him to feel the wind of its passage.

"What's the matter with you?" Frank yelled angrily. "Have you gone crazy?"

Joe's only response was a wordless bellow as he wound up to swing again.

"Joe!" Frank had to duck again as his brother launched another ferocious attack at him.

That's enough batting practice, Frank decided. This time, he didn't let Joe go into his follow-through with the shovel. He grabbed on to the wooden center pole, trying to yank the shovel out of Joe's hands.

Joe responded with a roar. The two brothers wrestled for control, holding the shovel at chest level, standing eye to eye.

That was when Frank noticed the tiny dart sticking out of the side of Joe's neck.

I guess I have my answer, he thought. They've shot him full of something. He *is* crazy. Frank wanted to remove the dart, but to do that would give Joe the shovel—and probably get him brained. He'd have to try another way.

"Joe!" Frank yelled into his brother's face. "Do you recognize me?"

It took a few shouts, but Joe finally responded. "Dead!" he shouted. "You're all dead!"

"What's this 'all' business?" Frank demanded. "There's just you, me, and the graveyard."

But Joe's eyes glared over his shoulder, scanning an apparently huge number of invisible enemies. "I see the dead all around us. Coming to get me. Get me for Iola. Let go of the shovel!"

Joe shook the handle so fiercely, he almost flung Frank away.

Frank managed to maintain his grip. "Who? What dead?"

Joe glanced toward a grave topped with a

soaring angel. "There. The Assassin who tried to kill me on the airplane. There—the race car driver who fell to his death while I chased him. Aaagh! Burned! Horrible!"

He looked in another direction. "The guys in the van who shot at us till we drove them off the road. They're here, too! With guns!" Joe tore the shovel from Frank's grasp and swung it at empty air. Then he whipped around and smashed the top of a gravestone.

Frank leapt for Joe's back and put his arms around Joe, pinning his younger brother's arms. Joe continued to grip the shovel, however.

"Do you know me?" Frank yelled in his brother's ear.

In the middle of trying to pull free, Joe suddenly stopped and looked over his shoulder at his brother. "Frank? It's really you?"

Then a deeper horror settled on Joe's face. "You're dead, too? She brought you after me?"

Joe tore free and swung the shovel again. Frank flung himself away before it could connect and landed flat on his back. Joe towered over him, raising the shovel for a two-handed blow.

I can't beat him, Frank thought, so I'd better distract him.

"Joe!" he yelled. "Behind you!"

Joe whipped around to swing his weapon at a series of enemies only he could see.

"Joe, I'm on your side," Frank yelled. "I won't let anyone get you."

"My side," Joe echoed in a quieter voice.

"Joe—" Frank tried to get up, only to narrowly miss getting his head smashed.

"Stay down!" Joe warned. "Maybe you're tricking me. You always liked Iola. You picked on me for making her feel bad!"

Frank stayed on the ground, and Joe concentrated his swings on some of his invisible enemies.

"Joe, the Iola who's been calling you isn't real. She's a clone—a look-alike created at the Lazarus Clinic."

"Lazarus?" Joe actually stopped in midswing.

"She's a fake, Joe. Whoever you've been seeing, they aren't real. I've been up to the Lazarus Clinic. I've seen a fake Gray Man, a fake Al-Rousasa . . ." His breath came in a sudden gasp. "A fake Callie!"

Frank hit his forehead with the heel of one hand. He couldn't believe that he had missed such an obvious clue! When they set off for Maine, Callie had given him her new scarf, and he dropped it at the hangar during the fight. He had it in his pocket now only because Matt had returned it. So how could Callie have been gagged with it when the blade fell?

I must have been really tired not to figure that one out, Frank thought. It was obvious that the clone masters had made a copy of Callie. They'd probably been pressed for time, since she'd gone to Maine on the spur of the moment. But they had surveillance pictures, fax machines, and probably a fast plane to bring in whatever they needed. The scarf that shouldn't have been there was just a detail lost in the rush.

They probably had their creation strapped to the table from the moment he and the real Callie entered the clinic. Then it was a case of grabbing his Callie and leading him to the clone. Suddenly he recalled hearing a voice calling his name when he had returned to the clinic. That must have been the real Callie!

"She's alive, Joe!" he yelled out in relief. "Alive!"

"Alive?" Joe said foggily. "Who?"

"Callie!" Frank shouted the name. "I don't know where they're holding her, but she's alive. I don't know where she is, but we can save her."

Joe stared down at Frank. "You're not making any sense. And we can't even save ourselves. Ghosts after us."

Despite the seriousness of the situation, Frank almost had to laugh at Joe's saying that *he* wasn't making any sense. Joe went back to battling imaginary demons. At least, Frank thought, he seems willing to think I'm alive now. If only I can get close enough to get that dart out of his neck! The longer it's there, the more demented he'll get.

"Joe, if Callie is alive, there must be a reason. Maybe the Assassins thought they'd need information from her to make this bizarre farce work better."

For a second, hope lit Joe's tortured face. "Mom? Could Mom still be alive?"

Frank was chilled. Their mother wasn't at home. Had she, too, fallen into the hands of the Assassins? The thought was more than he could deal with.

"I think so," he told Joe, silently praying that he was right.

Joe stopped swinging the shovel, and his eyes fixed on Frank with desperate intensity. "And Vanessa. She could still be alive, too?"

His voice held a pleading note that nearly broke Frank's heart. "Yes," Frank said. "They'd want her to tell them things, too. Things they couldn't find out—things that only the two of you would know. The Assassins would need that."

"Assassins!" Joe was back into his hallucinatory battle. "One of them's out there, the one who took poison rather than answer questions. Pale! Horrible! Rotting!"

Joe swung and chopped as though he were fighting for his life. Now Frank had to fight just as hard—for Joe's sanity.

"Listen to me!" Frank rose to his knees,

THE HARDY BOYS CASEFILES

risking a blow from the shovel. "Joe, they're not real. Can you touch them?"

Joe shuddered. "Don't want to. Dead. Rot. Slime." He looked beyond Frank and gagged. "Brains coming out."

"I tell you, they're not real. Do you feel it when your shovel hits them?"

Joe paused, his phantom-racked brain trying to think. "Sometimes," he said.

"That's because sometimes you're hitting gravestones when you swing," Frank said. He held up an arm. "Look. I'm real. Touch me."

Hesitantly, as if he feared a horrible trick, Joe reached out. "You're real. You're warm. Frank, you *are* alive!"

"I came all the way back from Maine to save you. Come on, Joe. It's up to us to save the others."

"Them?" Joe gestured in horror to the army of phantom figures he believed surrounded them.

"No, Joe. They're not real. We have real people to save. Mom. Callie. Vanessa."

"Iola says they're dead. Next they'll be coming to get me for her."

"Iola is fake, Joe. She's just somebody they've made to look like her. Remember how they did that before?"

Joe was trembling so badly, he dropped the shovel. "No. A ghost. She knows all about me. She knew what we said right before—

before she"—the word came out as a broken cry—"died."

Frank's mind raced. The other double had been programmed with all sorts of information from Iola's diaries. But where could the Assassin have learned about Iola and Joe's final argument? Then he had it!

"Joe, there was someone else who saw the whole thing. The girl you were talking to— what was her name? Viv? Val?"

"Val!" Joe nodded his head vigorously. "You're right! Smart Frank!" His eyes burned as he focused on Frank. "Iola's not a ghost?"

"No ghost," Frank assured him, slowly getting to his feet. "She's a fake. If she were a ghost would she need to shoot you full of crazy-juice?"

"Shoot me?" Joe echoed.

"Here." Still concerned that he would frighten Joe, Frank pointed at the dart imbedded in Joe's neck rather than reach over and pull it out. "Feel there."

Joe's hand went to the side of his neck. He discovered the dart and pulled it free. "What?" he said, completely baffled as he stared at it. "What?"

"Nice try," a voice said from behind them. "Very good indeed."

It was a bright voice, the voice of an eager young woman. It was also a voice that shouldn't have existed on earth anymore.

"Iola!" Joe cried. He turned to stare at her, then fell to his knees with a whimper.

The figure before them was dressed in gauzy white, with the pixie features and dark hair of Iola Morton. Looking at her a little critically, Frank noticed that although her voice was mocking, the face hardly moved.

"I see the Assassins still haven't managed to get rid of the stone-face effect with their facial surgery."

"It worked well enough to convince you that your Callie had died," the false Iola said.

"I was far enough away so I couldn't really see," Frank said. His eyes narrowed. "You sound like Iola and look like her, but I get the feeling you're a lot older."

Again, the double's voice dripped scorn, but her face remained immobile. "Did you think we would entrust work this important to an eighteen-year-old? I am considerably older. My specialty is psychological warfare. I had your brother well conditioned, yet you managed to break through. I compliment you on your good work. But I shall have to end it now."

Her hand, until then hidden in the gauzy gown, came up. The woman who looked like Iola Morton held a pistol.

And it was aimed at Frank Hardy's head.

Chapter

14

FRANK LOOKED FROM the muzzle of the gun in the imposter's hand toward Joe. His younger brother had fallen to his knees, tears streaming down his face.

"Your mistake was in trying to appeal to his intellect," the false Iola said smugly. "I control your brother by his emotions. As you can see, he's helpless. I can handle you first, then finish with him. By then he'll see the end as a kindness."

Some kindness, Frank thought.

"Before you do that," he said, "maybe you could answer a few questions that trouble me. Call it professional courtesy."

"I see no reason to be courteous to someone who's going to die so soon," the female terrorist said.

"This must have been quite an operation," Frank said, stalling for time. "From what Joe told me and what I saw, you have at least five doubles in your organization: you, Al-Rousasa, the Gray Man, our mother, Callie." His eyes narrowed. "I bet you even have a phony Vanessa."

The woman nodded. "You missed her very dramatic appearance on an adjustable underwater platform after we used a psychological trick to lure your brother to the waterfront. His response was most gratifying. "

Just keep talking, Frank thought. "Hard work should be appreciated," he continued. "These must have been a rough few months, getting everything ready. Going after us was a real crash project."

"Don't flatter yourself. Two of our transformed people are also planned for other assignments. It would be useful, shall we say, for an operative of Al-Rousasa's reputation to be in the field again. And the benefits from infiltrating our own Gray Man into the Network would be incalculable."

"So they just slapped the rest of you together."

Frank knew he was running the risk of a quick bullet in the brain, but he had to get the woman talking. It would buy him time, and maybe get some information.

"I spent weeks of operations to get 'slapped together,' as you put it," the false Iola said.

"So did our look-alike for Vanessa Bender. We shared the same hospital room."

"And Joe says our mother is dead. Did you clone her, too?"

That brought a hollow laugh from Iola. "I will satisfy your curiosity before you die. Your mother was only an unexpected intrusion in our plans. The woman your brother found supposedly murdered was an actress, hired for an expensive Halloween prank."

Frank nodded, forcing himself to keep his expression bland. In truth he was horrified that the Assassins would go to such great lengths to push both Joe and him over the edge.

"You did quite a job of switching people— Callie after we arrived at the clinic, and I guess my mother when she went out for candy."

The false Iola nodded. "We set the murder scenes very well. Even better, they disassembled quickly, so that all trace of the crimes would seem to disappear."

"Right down to a fresh layer of dust on the floor at the clinic. How did you do that? A reverse vacuum cleaner?"

"Close enough."

"When your people got Mom," Frank speculated, "they must have grabbed her just as she left the door. Then they had her keys to get in and plant those killer candles in the jack-o'-lanterns."

"We researched your family life extensively, especially regarding Halloween customs," the double said. "The candles wouldn't have killed you, but the toxins would have made you quite irrational."

"So we could discredit ourselves as witnesses in the Brubaker trial?"

"Exactly. We had several contingency plans, however. The major thrust was to drive your brother mad. Our best hope was to completely destroy his credibility as a prosecution witness by having him appear to murder you."

The Iola clone sounded a little angry that things hadn't turned out according to her plan. "That was the reason for the Bender girl's apparent death and the whole psychological war on your brother. You were to be lured up to Maine, led to make a fool of yourself with the police, and then eliminated. Your dead body would be shipped back here, and the murder weapon would be found in Joe's hand. We knew, though, that even if you weren't eliminated, we would have ruined your credibility on the witness stand."

"All very complicated," Frank said. "For one thing, it depended on the Assassins' always knowing where we were."

"We had microtransmitters planted on both of you—although, I regret to say, we lost your signal somehow."

Frank remembered the bruising fall down

the gully after he'd escaped from the clinic. Apparently, the bug they had placed on him had either been torn off in the underbrush or destroyed by the fall.

"Well, you got me in the end. I'm afraid this will be messy, though. What are you going to do with the people you kidnapped?"

"Oh, we have a disposal system all worked out," the evil double assured Frank. "Now, enough questions!" She raised the gun in a two-handed shooting stance.

Instinctively Frank threw himself on the ground, but no shot came. The false Iola had been knocked down by a shovel swung at knee level.

"Fake!" Joe Hardy cried, throwing the shovel away to pummel the woman. "Miserable, lousy, lying *fake!*"

Frank leapt up and pulled his brother off the woman. "She's out cold, Joe. Clipped her head on a gravestone when she fell."

Joe nodded, his expression grim. "Ghosts don't get knocked out." His eyes were clearer, more rational now. "A fake. All this time, she was playing with my head."

"No more, Joe," Frank said. "I promise that. Is anybody else around here? Where were you when the dart hit?"

Joe's hand went to the small wound on his neck. "I thought I'd been bitten by bats when I went into the mausoleum."

He rose, slinging the unconscious form of

the female terrorist over his shoulder, and led Frank through the glowing mist. The ghostly lighting effect was just that—an effect. They nearly stumbled over a cable for one of the lights as they approached the Morton mausoleum.

Frank had taken the precaution of picking up the false Iola's gun. Now he paused at the entrance. "If someone's in there, they'll be on guard," he said. "Ready to shoot first and ask questions later."

"They may not shoot if they see a friend," Joe said. He swung the limp form of the Iola clone in front of him and moved her into the doorway. Frank followed noiselessly.

The mausoleum was dark, but the Hardys smelled a rich odor of tobacco smoke. "Margit, is that you?" a husky voice asked.

Standing behind Joe, Frank had a brief glimpse of a little kid in a Death costume. Or was it a kid? What Frank had first thought was a mask was actually the wrinkled face of an elderly midget. The gun in the man's hand was no kid's toy, either.

Still holding the female terrorist before him, Joe rushed across the burial chamber. The little man whipped his pistol up, but Joe was now close enough to hurl Iola's double into the man. The two fell to the floor of the mausoleum, the midget caught in the folds of gauze.

Frank jumped forward to kick the gun away, aiming the gun that had been Iola's at the man. "Give it up," he said. "You can't get away."

The man looked at Frank, then Joe. Then suddenly a spasm of pain came over the man's wrinkled face, and his tiny body went into convulsions.

Frank tore the still-unconscious double off the midget's body, but already the man was dead.

"I thought it was a kid," Joe said in horror, looking down.

"No, he was an adult, no matter what his height was." Frank shook his head. "I suppose it would be very useful for terrorists to have someone working for them who could pass for a child."

Joe nodded. "Bombs in schoolbags, shots in the back." His face twisted. "Messages delivered by trick-or-treaters."

"And bugs planted," Frank said. "Remember the kid who bumped into us as we walked to the marina? A very sophisticated delivery system."

He knelt and examined the man's body. He opened the man's mouth. "Poison capsule in a false tooth," he said. "If we weren't sure before, we can be sure the Assassins are in it now."

"Yeah," Joe said. "Nobody takes an Assassin alive."

The boys stood in silence, a silence suddenly interrupted by a faint noise from an open sarcophagus. Frank went over to check it out. The stone receptacle didn't hold a dead body, but a prisoner.

His mother lay there, bound and gagged.

Then Frank did a double take. The woman wasn't his mother, although she would have passed for Mrs. Hardy on first glance. This woman's facial features were a little sharper, though, and she was thinner. Still, she had the same blue eyes, now wide with fear over her gagged mouth.

Incoherent hums bubbled through the gag.

Frank pulled out his pocketknife and went to work on the ropes and gag.

"They were going to kill me!" the woman burst out when Frank got her free. Joe joined them, to help the woman out of the cold stone box. "I'm Lorna Friel, by the way."

"You didn't expect to get this far into your role, I'm sure," Frank said, taking her by the arm and leading her out of the mausoleum. Joe followed.

The actress nodded. "I was told it was a joke, a Halloween surprise, although making myself up as a corpse didn't seem in the best of taste. On the other hand, these people were willing to pay a fortune. Apparently, I looked just like the guest of honor for this party."

"Except there was no party," Frank said.

Lorna nodded. "That's right. I was brought to some house and led up to the attic. But only one person came in." She nodded. "Your friend over there."

"Actually, he's my brother," Frank said. "And he thought you were our mother— murdered."

The actress stared at Joe, her eyes full of horror. "That wasn't what I was told."

"Of course not. What happened after Joe left?"

"These people came up to the attic and hustled me out. I told them something had gone very wrong, but they seemed delighted with the way things were going. When I threatened to quit, they pulled guns, tied me up, and brought me to the cemetery."

Lorna Friel shook her head. "The setup here was weird. They had lights rigged outside, a cage full of bats, and some kind of dart gun. The little guy released the bats and shot your brother."

She looked at Joe. "Then you ran out of here like a crazy man. The little guy wanted to kill me, but the girl seemed to be the boss. She told him to hold on to me in case they needed something more."

"You were lucky," Frank said grimly. "They killed one of their own people in front of my eyes."

He leaned forward. "Now think carefully. While you were their prisoner, did these two mention anyone else? Did they say where they were?"

Lorna Friel nodded, her blue eyes wide with horror. "The little man kept telling me they had a basement full of loose ends, four of them, north of town. He kept laughing about it, saying his boss had even had them imported from Maine to their headquarters here."

She shook her head. "He said they'd all go through the mill north of here before daybreak."

Chapter

15

JOE FROWNED. "Maybe it's just that junk they shot me full of, but that makes no sense at all to me."

"I can't tell you what it means," Lorna Friel responded. "That was all the man said."

" 'Through the mill,' " Frank repeated. "And he said it was north of here?"

"That's right," the actress said. "I didn't understand, but I was in no position to ask any questions."

"I may have it," Frank said, turning to Joe. "Remember Greengage Textiles?"

"Sure. There was a time when half the north side of town worked for them," Joe said. "Then the company closed its plant. That was a long time ago. We were just little kids."

"So little that you forget what people used to call the plant—Greengage Mills."

Joe's eyebrows rose. "It's worth checking out."

"But first we have some business here that needs our attention." The Iola Morton clone was still unconscious. Frank walked over to her and knelt down. He pinched her mouth open, then reached inside. "She has a false tooth, too," he said.

"Is anything about her real?" Joe muttered, glaring down at the woman yet feeling guilty. It was a weird situation, having a deadly enemy who looked just like someone you loved.

But then, this whole night had been a succession of weird and frightening situations.

"I'd say this was real." Frank delicately removed a small white object from the woman's mouth, then shook a tiny capsule into his palm. "Real poison."

"Best description of her I've ever heard," Joe said.

He tried to fight off a yawn, but it overcame him and he stretched. "Guess I'm coming back to reality," he said sheepishly. "Every part of my body hurts, and I'm exhausted."

Frank's expression was concerned as he turned to his brother. "You sure you're okay?"

That got a laugh out of Joe. "I feel about as good as you look."

Frank ran a hand through his matted dark hair, wincing as he did so. "I see what you mean," he admitted. "Neither of us is in much shape to launch a rescue mission."

"But it has to be us," Joe said grimly. "The police aren't going to listen to what we say. Not after I reported Mom's death." He quickly told Frank what had happened.

Lorna Friel looked even more guilty. "If there's something I can do to help . . ."

"Maybe there is," Frank said. "Let's just finish up here."

They used the rope that had bound the actress to restrain and gag the false Iola, or rather Margit, as the now dead guard had called her. Then Frank searched his brother's clothes inch by inch until he found what he'd been looking for. It was a tiny construction about the size of a straight pin, with a slightly larger glassy bulb at one end.

"Going to stomp on it?" Joe asked.

Frank shook his head and slipped the pinpoint into one of the gauzy layers of the phony Iola's dress. "We're going to leave this right here so the other Assassins will think this is where you are." Then he picked up the body of the Iola clone and carried it into the mausoleum.

When Frank returned he handed Joe the guard's gun. "I guess we're ready," he said. "Let's take the van. We can come back for Callie's car later."

They piled into the van, Frank at the wheel, Joe in the passenger's seat, and Lorna in the back. They glided through the silent late-night streets.

Joe glanced at his watch. Five o'clock, the dead of night. Just the time to be leaving a graveyard.

Frank drove toward the northern end of town. Most of the houses were old and not well kept. Development had been slow to come to the north side. Two other abandoned mills in another part of town had been turned into expensive condominiums.

But the biggest mill, Greengage, hadn't been renovated. It was part of a deserted industrial area, its redbrick walls gaunt and worn.

"Lovely place," Joe said, staring out his window as they drove up to it. "It looks like a standing advertisement on the dangers of industrialization."

"Well, this is what these places look like before the developers make them 'quaint,' " Frank said, stopping the van on the road.

"It could be pretty, I suppose," Joe conceded. "Look, the place even has a waterwheel and its own stream."

"Where inconvenient prisoners can be disposed of," Frank said grimly.

"I get it," Joe said. "Sent through the mill."

His eyes suddenly narrowed. The windows

of the mill had been painted over, but Joe thought he saw light at the corner of a small basement window by the waterwheel. "Am I crazy, or is that a light?"

Frank looked in the direction Joe was pointing. "Definitely a light," Frank said. "They must be down there."

"I think you're right," Joe said. "Let's work out a plan."

A very nervous Lorna Friel sat in the back of the van, listening as the boys developed their plan of attack. She grew more nervous when they explained her part in it.

"You're sure I won't get in trouble for doing this?" she said worriedly when they drove off.

Frank pulled the van up by a pay phone in front of an all-night diner. "You'll be telling the truth about the mill, as far as it goes. Somebody is living in it illegally."

Joe nodded. "And after we get back there, the cops will be sure to find a loud and dangerous party in progress."

"I don't know," Lorna said.

Joe turned to her. "You said you'd like to help us. Well, this is the help we need. We can't go to the police with a report of what's really going on. They'd either think we were kidding or they'd lock us in padded cells."

"Either way, we won't be able to help the people being held in the mill," Frank said.

"But if you call as a worried housewife, the

police will respond and we'll get the backup we need.'' Joe smiled at her. ''Think of it as an acting job.''

''Okay,'' the actress said. ''I'll do it.''

They dropped her off with lots of change. ''Give us five minutes, then call the cops,'' Joe said. ''You can stay in the diner until things settle down.''

They drove back to the mill through a pre-dawn haze. ''Halloween is almost over,'' Frank said, looking up at the slightly brightening sky.

Joe's face was grim as he checked over the gun that had belonged to the Assassin. ''Let's hope we don't have to deal with any more ghosts.''

Frank pulled off the road a short distance past the mill. They headed for the main gate.

''Hmm. Old gate, old paint, but a new chain and lock,'' Frank said.

''A *loose* chain,'' Joe said, stretching the links to their limit between the two door halves. ''A person can—ouch!—squeeze through.''

They went across a silent and overgrown loading area, climbed up on the old loading dock, and found that one of the sealed metal shutters had been cut through.

''Welder's torch,'' Frank said, fingering the twisted end of the shutter. ''Whoever got in here wasn't fooling around.''

''We knew that about them from the beginning,'' Joe muttered as they crept into the building.

Sneaking through echoing galleries where huge machines once had stood, they searched for a way to the basement.

Following a barely noticeable glimmer of light, Joe found a stairway. Halfway down, the stairwell was masked by a ragged blanket, hiding the flickering glow of lamplight below.

Quietly Joe stepped to the blanket and twitched it aside for a quick peek. The basement was a dirty place. Rows of low, thick pillars divided the huge basement into compartments.

''I guess they needed all those pillars to support the weight of the machinery upstairs,'' Frank whispered, ''but they make our job tougher. If we're right and everyone is down here, the Assassins would have had to split them up into different compartments. We'll have to move fast to get them all.''

''Then we'll move fast,'' Joe said.

''Let me check things out first,'' Frank said. ''If someone's lying in wait for us, it's better if we separate.''

Joe nodded in agreement. He held the curtain aside and Frank slipped past. The first compartment was empty. But sticking out from the next compartment Frank could see a pair of legs in black jeans with ropes around the ankles.

Callie! Frank thought excitedly. He pulled out his knife and silently crept forward.

A few minute later, Frank reported back to Joe. "Callie's safe," he whispered, his voice expressing his relief. "They must have brought her back after I escaped, figuring they could use her to make me think I was seeing ghosts. I cut her free, but I told her to stay there until we've located everyone. The Gray Man is two compartments away. I slipped the knife to him."

"What about guards?" Joe asked.

"I heard someone moving around at the far end of the basement," Frank said, "so I know there's at least one. But there are so many pillars I couldn't tell if there are any more guards or not."

"I'm coming with you to check it out," Joe said.

"Okay," Frank said. "Follow me." As the boys crept down an aisle created by the pillars, a familiar figure in a trench coat appeared in front of them.

"Loose already?" Joe whispered.

Frank pointed to the nasty set of scratches across the Gray Man's face. "That's the cheap imitation. I did that to him."

The phony government man pulled out a gun, and Frank and Joe dived behind one of the wide pillars. The gunshot rang out deafeningly in the basement. Then came a yell, followed by a muffled call of "All clear."

It was the Gray Man's voice, but in the cavernous basement the voice was muted, and even Frank couldn't be sure which Gray Man was speaking. The Hardys looked at each other. "Cover me," Joe whispered. Just then another shot rang out.

Joe raced from one pillar to the next, looking for the two Gray Men. Frank remained behind another pillar, watching Joe's movements, prepared to fire off a warning shot to keep any guards from advancing.

Joe crept into a compartment and found two Gray Men, one on the ground, apparently dead, the other standing over him, gun in hand. The gun toter turned to Joe.

He had a bruise on his face, but no scratches.

"Good to see you," the Gray Man said. Leaving his clone lying on the floor, he dashed into the next compartment. Someone fired at him, but the bullet hit a pillar.

Joe joined the agent, followed by Frank. They found the Gray Man cutting their mother loose. Frank stood guard until his mother was free.

"One more prisoner, two more terrorists," the Gray Man said. "A blond girl, and a man they remade to look like Al-Rousasa. They've been at the far end making plans, but now they have a problem. They can't get past us, and the stairway at the end has fallen to rubble, so they're trapped."

"But they have a hostage," Joe said grimly. "Vanessa."

"Listen!" A slightly accented man's voice came from the far end of the basement. "We have guns and the girl. You let us go, or she dies."

"She dies, you *never* get out of here alive," Joe shouted back. "I'll burn this place over you if I have to."

"You don't dare," the Al-Rousasa clone sneered.

"You got the voice right," Joe called. "Too bad you couldn't get the brain, too."

"We are coming out, the girl first. If you shoot, I will shoot her," the terrorist yelled.

A very frightened-looking Vanessa Bender appeared in the narrow aisle. She was unbound, but the Al-Rousasa clone's pistol was pointed at her head. "All of you—out of that compartment!" he screamed. "And throw down your guns."

Joe came out into the aisle first. He knew if they surrendered, they were dead. He also knew that he wasn't a good enough shot to hit the terrorist without endangering Vanessa. I hope I'm doing the right thing, he thought. He threw down his gun, sending it skittering across the stone floor.

The imitation Al-Rousasa turned his attention to the sound for a fraction of a second. And the Gray Man fired.

With a horrible cry, the terrorist flew backward. He had been hit in the shoulder. Vanessa grabbed for his gun as he fell. A slim female arm came from behind the pillar and dragged Vanessa back into a compartment.

Joe turned to Frank. "You take care of Mom and Callie. I'll handle this."

Joe raced toward the last compartment. There he found two girls struggling on the floor. Both had ash blond hair and both wore almost identical clothes. Both held guns in their right hands, while gripping the wrist of their opponent's gun hand with their left.

When they saw Joe, both cried, "Help me get her!"

How could he tell which was the girl he knew and which was the trained killer? There's only one way to prove this, he thought.

"You'll have to shoot me first," Joe said.

Chapter

16

THE TWO VANESSAS looked astonished.

"What do you mean?" one of them asked.

"Whichever one of you is the fake," Joe said evenly, "will have to shoot to get past me. You and your people took too much from me tonight. You're going to pay for that."

Joe took a step forward, and everything happened at once. The second Vanessa suddenly broke free from her mirror image. "Joe, look out!" she shouted.

Joe ducked behind a pillar just as the first Vanessa leveled her gun at him and fired, but her shot went wild. Before she could fire again, a gun butt slammed into the back of her head. She fell to the floor in a crumpled heap.

"I couldn't shoot her," Vanessa Bender said nervously.

"What you did worked just fine," Joe told her, coming out from behind the pillar. He took her in his arms and held her tightly. "You don't know how glad I am to see you." His voice was thick with emotion. "I thought—"

"I know," Vanessa said softly.

"You two want some privacy?" Frank Hardy teased. He was standing a few feet behind them, one arm around Mrs. Hardy, the other around Callie. The Gray Man stood behind them.

"Later, definitely." Joe gave Vanessa a squeeze, then ran to hug his mother. "You pick the strangest places to shop for candy."

Mrs. Hardy ruffled his hair. "I love you, too," she said softly.

The police arrived ten minutes after the battle, and Network agents alerted by the Gray Man on a portable phone belonging to the Assassins arrived shortly after the police. The authorities swarmed all over, taking away the two remaining terrorists and searching for weapons and other Assassin paraphernalia. The police called the fire marshal to tell him that Vanessa Bender had been found alive and well. Vanessa was relieved to learn the marshal had not yet located her mother in Europe.

Mrs. Hardy and a proud Lorna Friel were

giving their statements, while Frank and Callie stood to one side watching.

"Miss me?" Callie asked.

"More than that," Frank replied. "I thought I'd lost you forever. I should have realized they'd stick a double on that table. It just goes to show how upset and tired I was. Matt, the mechanic at the airport, gave me your scarf. It seems I lost it during the fight in the hangar. Yet you, uh, *she* was gagged with it on the death table."

Frank winced as he remembered the scene at the Lazarus Clinic. He told her the gruesome tale of the clone.

Callie shook her head and shuddered. "They killed her. How could they do that?"

"The problem is, they find it very easy to do." Frank's face grew stern. "That's why we have to keep trying to stop them."

Callie nodded in agreement.

"Callie, when I thought you had died because of me—" Frank's voice failed.

"Remember what I said at the airport. It came with the territory when I started dating you." She held him close. "And I haven't regretted it. Not one day."

"Maybe now *you* two need some privacy," Joe Hardy said.

Frank simply grinned.

"The Gray Man wants to talk to us." Joe shot an apologetic glance at Callie. "Alone."

"I'll go keep Vanessa company," she said.

"But don't make us wait too long." Callie looked around at all the law officers. "There are a few good-looking—"

"Don't even think about it," Frank said. He couldn't help smiling as he and Joe walked across the basement to join the Gray Man.

"I've never come so close to losing so much," he told his younger brother. "Makes me appreciate everything all the more."

"I know what you mean."

"So," said the Gray Man. He stood by a rusted file cabinet, puffing casually on a cigarette, blowing the smoke up to the ceiling. "Have you two figured it all out yet?"

"I've got part of it," Joe offered. "The Assassins wanted Frank and me to lose all credibility for the Brubaker case." The Gray Man nodded. "But why did they especially pick on me?"

"It's pretty awful," Frank said, "but I think they took advantage of the fact that you had already had one girlfriend die. They thought they could push you over the edge by making you think Vanessa was dead and then bringing Iola back into your life."

"That's right," the Gray Man said. "And they knew more about you and your late girlfriend than you can imagine." The Gray Man pulled a file folder from one of the opened drawers. "This contains a detailed account of the day Iola died, right down to the dialogue between you two. Some of these other folders contain photos and information on your friends and family. There's even a picture of your house from last Halloween.''

Frank stared at the photo, noting the pottery jack-o'-lanterns in the windows. "They really did their homework." He could barely mask the anger in his voice.

Joe put a hand on Frank's shoulder. "I know how you feel," he said quietly. "They really got inside my head, too."

"But what about the hired actress for Mom?" Joe asked.

"She was part of their contingency plans. They had people on tap to play everybody in your family." The government man showed them another file folder, with actors' résumés and photos of people who looked like Fenton Hardy, Aunt Gertrude, even some of their other friends. "When your mother came home unexpectedly, they put their plan right into gear."

The Gray Man produced some candles from a box on a nearby table. "Drugging you, as well as the psychological warfare, was, you'll have to admit, very effective. They didn't have to kill you, only wear you down. The idea was to make you act crazy."

"But why go through all this?" Joe asked. "Why didn't they just kill us?"

"Discrediting us would be better than killing us," Frank said. "Our depositions would be used in the trial anyway, if we had been killed. But imagine what a sharp defense attorney could do to us on the stand. We'd have to admit we'd apparently lied to the police in two states, inventing murders.''

Frank glanced at Joe. "One of us might even be up on a murder charge.''

" 'While not of sound mind,' " Joe said grimly. "I'd have been useless as a witness.''

"You're right," the Gray Man said. "If our star witnesses could be dismissed as loonies, the whole case would have gone up in smoke.'' The Gray Man took a last drag on his cigarette, then put it out. "Devious, don't you think?''

"And they grabbed you because you helped compile the information and spearheaded the whole operation," Joe said.

"They grabbed me soon after Frank called. My clone would have gone on the stand, made a valiant effort to save the case, but lose. Then he'd be in my job, while I was six feet under.''

"Well, it's all over now." Joe sighed. "Although I don't know how we're going to explain all this to Vanessa, Callie, and Mom.''

"You won't." The Gray Man signaled for one of his agents to come over and stand by the files. "No one, including the boys in blue, gets the whole story," he told the man. Then he led the Hardys toward the staircase.

"We'll handle the police and the media,''

he said. "By this afternoon most of this will not have happened."

"But people were kidnapped," Joe blurted out.

"By a third-rate criminal gang." The Gray Man had a smirk on his face. "They were going to ask for a ransom, but their plans fell apart."

Joe shook his head, torn between disbelief and admiration. "You guys can certainly rewrite history."

"Sometimes it's necessary," the Gray Man said.

"And what are you going to tell the police in Maine?" Frank asked.

"That the Frank Hardy who contacted them was a fake." The Gray Man signaled another of his agents, who led Mrs. Hardy, Vanessa, and Callie over to them.

"I suggest you all get some rest. It's been a trying night." With that he dismissed the group and went to join the local police.

"Where to?" Frank asked once the group was outside.

A bright orange and yellow sun was rising in the east. Birds soared overhead, and a gentle breeze rustled the autumn leaves.

"It's six-seventeen," Joe said, looking at his watch. "Anybody know a good place where hungry people could get a stack of pancakes and a gallon of orange juice?"

"*Starving* is more the word," Callie said, and Vanessa agreed.

"How about breakfast at our house?" Mrs. Hardy offered. "Pancakes, ham, the works."

"Great, Mom." A gleam appeared in Joe Hardy's eyes. "I know we missed Halloween. But I'm a good boy and eat all my food." Joe grinned from ear to ear. "May I have some candy?"

Laughing, they all piled into the boys' van. Frank smiled. Next stop—home.

Frank and Joe's next case:

An urgent call for help from their father's friend chemist Sam Gentle has drawn Frank and Joe across the country to northern Arizona. The cryptic message offers no clue to the danger he's in, and it's one secret he will never reveal. Soon after their arrival, the boys find Sam Gentle lying at the bottom of Wolf's Tooth Canyon—a victim of murder.

The Hardys suspect that Sam's research at Titan Chemical Industries led to a discovery that turned him into a target for terror. But his death was only the beginning. The chemist left behind a deadly hidden legacy, and Frank and Joe are all that stands between the killer and Sam's daughter, Tiffany . . . in *Sheer Terror*, Case #81 in the Hardy Boys Casefiles™.